"Nothing Wrong With My Ego."
"Nothing But Its Size."

His only response was a smug smile.

Sally shook her head ruefully, finding it difficult to associate this man with the one she knew as her boss. He looked so relaxed. Nothing at all like the micromanaging, nitpicking tyrant she knew from the office.

Her gaze settled on his chest and her thoughts slipped to the previous night. She remembered the weight of his body on hers, her breasts flattened beneath his chest, his legs twined with hers.

He'd kissed her.

Not a real kiss, she reminded herself. Not the passionate kind at any rate. It had lasted no more than a second or two. But she wondered what it would feel like if Vince *really* kissed her.

Dear Reader,

The saga of the six Vietnam Vets and the missing pieces of paper continues with the story of Preacher's son...as do the stranger-than-fiction happenings I've experienced while writing this series.

After the release of the first book in the series, which was dedicated to David "Babyson" Davidson, I received a telephone call from a woman. Imagine my shock when she introduced herself as Dave's mother! Prior to purchasing the book, she knew nothing about me, had never met my husband and had no idea the book she'd bought earlier that morning was dedicated to her son, until she returned home and began to read. It was truly by chance that she'd chosen my book from the hundreds that line the shelves and a miracle that she was able to track me down! It was a thrill to visit with her over the phone, and my husband and I hope to have the pleasure of meeting her in person very soon.

As I continue to write the soldiers' stories, I can't help but wonder what stranger-than-life experience will be waiting for me around the next corner....

Peggy Moreland

PEGGY MORELAND

THE TEXAN'S BUSINESS PROPOSITION

Silhouette®

Desire

Published by Silhouette Books

America's Publisher of Contemporary Romance

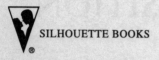

SILHOUETTE BOOKS

®

ISBN-13: 978-0-373-76796-0
ISBN-10:   0-373-76796-X

THE TEXAN'S BUSINESS PROPOSITION

Copyright © 2007 by Peggy Bozeman Morse

This edition published by arrangement with Harlequin Books S.A.

Visit Silhouette Books at www.eHarlequin.com

Printed in U.S.A.

Recent Books by Peggy Moreland

Silhouette Desire

*Five Brothers and a Baby #1532
*Baby, You're Mine #1544
*The Last Good Man in Texas #1580
*Sins of a Tanner #1616
*Tanner Ties #1676
†The Texan's Forbidden Affair #1718
†The Texan's Convenient Marriage #1736
†The Texan's Honor-Bound Promise #1750
Merger of Fortunes #1771
†The Texan's Business Proposition #1796

Silhouette Books

*Tanner's Millions

*The Tanners of Texas
†A Piece of Texas

PEGGY MORELAND

published her first romance with Silhouette Books in 1989 and continues to delight readers with stories set in her home state of Texas. Peggy is a winner of a National Readers' Choice Award, a nominee for the *Romantic Times BOOKreviews* Reviewer's Choice Award and a two-time finalist for the prestigious RITA® Award, and her books frequently appear on the *USA TODAY* and Waldenbooks's bestseller lists. When not writing, Peggy can usually be found outside, tending the cattle, goats and other critters on the ranch she shares with her husband. You may write to Peggy at P.O. Box 1099, Florence, TX 76527-1099, or e-mail her at peggy@peggymoreland.com.

For Justin and Cassie

The best things in life are worth waiting on...
and y'all waited long enough! May love, happiness
and friendship accompany you throughout your lives.

Prologue

"In war, there are no unwounded soldiers."
—José Narosky

September 9, 1971

Preacher lay on his cot, his hands folded behind his head, staring at the shadowed canvas roof overhead. Though it was well past midnight and he was exhausted from a day spent on patrol, sleep evaded him.

From the far distance came the muffled rumble of bombs exploding. Closer was the not-so-muffled sound of snoring.

He shot a frown at the cot next to his and considered giving it a swift kick and telling his bunkmate to turn over…but decided against it. Just because he couldn't sleep didn't mean Fast Eddie had to join in his misery.

Fast Eddie. He snorted a laugh at the irony of the nickname. There was nothing fast about Eddie. He talked slow, walked slow. But the nickname assigned him during boot camp had stuck, the same as Preacher's. Preacher's real name was Vincent Donnelly, but it had been so long since he'd been called by his given name, he doubted he would respond if he were to hear it now.

The tag wasn't one he would've chosen for himself, but he'd take it any day of the week over "Coward", which is what some of the guys called him behind his back. He didn't like the name *or* what it signified. He wasn't a coward. He just had a hard time wrapping his mind around killing another human being.

Giving up on sleeping, he rolled from his cot and to his feet, hoping a walk might silence the chatter in his head. Once outside, he paused to look around. At the far end of the camp's perimeter fencing he saw a shadowed form in the bunker and headed that way, thinking he'd shoot the breeze for a while with whoever was pulling guard duty. As he neared the bunker, he heard the metallic click of a safety being released and called quickly, "It's me. Preacher."

He heard another click, indicating the safety was shoved back into place, and released a nervous breath.

"Figured it was you, Preacher."

Recognizing the deep voice as that of Pops, their team leader, he crossed to the bunker and settled down alongside his friend.

"Quiet night?" he asked.

Pops nodded, his gaze on the tall grasses that spread from the western corner of their camp. "Heard something a while ago. Thought we might have some company, but haven't seen or heard anything since."

"Could've been an animal. We spotted some wild dogs this afternoon on our way back to camp."

"Maybe."

Hearing the doubt in Pops's voice, Preacher glanced his way. "You think somebody's out there?"

Pops lifted a shoulder but kept his gaze on the grass beyond the fence. "Safer to think there is than get caught unprepared."

Preached nodded gravely.

They sat a long moment in silence before Pops slanted a look Preacher's way. "Still having trouble sleeping?"

Embarrassed by what some might consider a weakness, Preacher ducked his head. "Yeah. Can't seem to stop the chattering in my head."

"Chattering?"

"You know. Like two sides of my brain are carrying on a conversation."

"Have you tried telling them to shut up?"

Chuckling, Preacher shook his head. "Haven't tried that one yet."

"Do what I do," Pops suggested. "When I lay down at night, I close my eyes and picture home, my wife curled up beside me in bed. Relaxes my mind, my soul."

"Wouldn't work for me. When I think about home, it just adds more worries to the chatter already going on in my head. Things like is Karen managing okay without me? Has Vince cut his first tooth?"

Pops shifted his rifle to his left hand and slung an arm around Preacher's shoulders. "You worry too much, Preacher. You've got to learn to let some of that go. Have faith that your boy will survive cutting his first tooth the same as you and every other kid in the world has. And trust your wife to handle things while you're gone. She's capable isn't she?"

"You bet she is. Karen might look fragile, but she's tough. And Vince…well, he's pretty tough, too." He glanced Pops's way. "Did I tell you he's started climbing out of his crib? Karen told me about it in her last letter."

Pops withdrew his arm. "Next thing you know, he'll be driving a car."

Preacher held up a hand. "Please. Don't be putting those kinds of images in my mind. I can find enough to worry about as it is."

Chuckling, Pops pushed to his feet and stretched. "I need to take a leak. Mind standing guard for me?"

Preacher took the rifle Pops offered him. "Might as well. Can't sleep, anyway."

After Pops left to relieve himself, Preacher settled the rifle over the edge of the bunker and began slowly sweeping his gaze along the shadowed sea of swaying grass before him, while keeping his ear tuned to pick up the slightest sound. He'd made one full sweep and started a second when he heard a muffled sound behind him. He leaped to his feet, bringing the rifle up into position, its butt braced against his shoulder. With the nose of the barrel pointed in the direction the noise had come, he waited, listening.

After what seemed like an eternity, a twig snapped, the sound like a crack of thunder in the silence. Telling himself that it was probably just Pops returning, Preacher eased forward, moving stealthily in the direction the sound had come. He wanted badly to call out to Pops, verify that he was the one who had made the noise, but training and field experience had taught him the danger of revealing his position to a possible enemy.

A cold sweat beaded his forehead and upper lip, ran in a narrow rivulet down his spine. He paused a moment to drag his arm across his face to clear the moisture from his eyes, then moved on. When he reached the latrine, he flattened his back against the bamboo fence that surrounded it and waited, listening, his rifle held tight against his chest. Ten seconds. Twenty. Sweat dripped from his face, soaked the back of his undershirt. Thirty. Forty.

Keeping his movements slow and easy, he leaned to peer around the opening into the latrine. Ice filled his veins at the scene before him. Pops lay sprawled on the ground, still as death, while a Vietcong, dressed in the standard black pajamas the enemy wore, straddled him. The Vietcong lifted a hand high, and moonlight bounced off the blade of the knife he clutched.

Preacher opened his mouth to yell at the man to stop, to let Pops go. But no sound came out. Frozen by fear, he watched in what seemed like slow motion, as the hand started down, the tip of the blade aimed at Pops' chest.

The chatter started in his head again, one of the voices his own, the other that of the rancher who had bought him and his buddies a drink in the Texas bar, prior to them beginning the first leg of their journey for Vietnam.

"You boys scared?" the rancher asked bluntly.

"Yes, sir," Preacher admitted. "I've never shot a man before. Not sure I can."

The smile the rancher offered Preacher was filled with understanding, his wink that of a father reassuring his son. "Oh, I 'magine you'll find it easy enough, once those Vietcong start shooting at you."

But the rancher was wrong, Preacher thought as he watched the blade slowly arc down, drawing nearer and nearer Pops's chest. Pops, the man who had trained Preacher, stood by him, defended him when the other's had called him a coward, was about to die, and Preacher couldn't pull the trigger to save him.

He can't die, Preacher thought desperately. Not here, not like this. He had a wife waiting for him at home, a baby on the way.

Setting his jaw, he yanked the rifle to his shoulder and looked down the barrel, fixing the Vietcong's head between the cross-hairs. But as much as he wanted to save Pops' life, he couldn't bring himself to pull the trigger.

Anger built inside him, a red-hot inferno that fired his blood, roared in his ears. Taking the stock of the rifle in one hand and the barrel in the other, he opened his mouth and charged. The feral sound that spewed from deep inside him ripped through the night air like a machete. Before the Vietcong had time to react,

Preacher dropped the rifle over his head and jerked it back against his throat.

The Vietcong flew backward, losing his grip on the knife. The weapon hit the ground less than a foot from Preacher's boot and he kicked it out of reach. Before the man could scramble up, Preacher swung the rifle up to his shoulder and aimed it at the Vietcong's face. He saw the hate in the man's eyes…but not a trace of fear.

Behind him Pops moaned, stirred. Preacher started to glance back, wanting to make sure that Pops was all right, but as he did the Vietcong slid a hand beneath his shirt.

Fearing the man had a weapon concealed beneath the black tunic, Preacher stabbed the nose of his rifle against the Vietcong's chest. "Don't move!"

His lip curled in a sneer, the Vietcong ignored Preacher's order. Preacher saw the butt of a handgun appear a split second before its nose was pointed at him.

The blast that followed was deafening, echoing around and around the fenced area. Preacher stumbled back a step, his gaze frozen on the Vietcong's face. He saw the surprise that lit the man's eyes, watched as the life slowly faded from them. He glanced down at the man's chest where blood oozed from a gaping hole and gulped back the nausea that rose to his throat.

He heard a shout from outside the fenced latrine and knew the shot had raised an alarm in camp. The pounding of feet that followed assured him the soldiers were up and assuming their positions.

A hand lit on his shoulder, squeezed. He knew without looking it was Pops.

"You okay?" Pops asked.

Preacher swallowed hard, nodded. "Yeah. You?"

"Knot on my head is all, thanks to you. A second more and he would have slit my throat."

Fast Eddie appeared in the opening to the latrine, half-dressed, his feet bare. "Y'all okay?"

Pops nodded, then gestured toward the Vietcong sprawled on the ground. "Enemy penetrated our perimeter. Order a full sweep of camp to make sure he was alone, then check on the guards on duty. I'll get a detail together to take care of the body when I'm done here."

Fast Eddie looked from the dead Vietcong to the rifle that Preacher held, and his eyes shot wide. "You made the kill, Preacher?"

Preacher opened his mouth, then closed it and dropped his chin.

"You have your orders, soldier," Pops said tersely.

Fast Eddie snapped to attention. "Yes, sir." He took one last look at Preacher, then turned and jogged away.

Preacher squeezed his eyes shut, but the image of the man lying at his feet with his life's blood pouring from his chest remained fixed on the back of his lids. He'd killed one man to save the life of another. What gave him the right to decide who lived and who died? He wasn't God.

As if reading Preacher's mind, Pops tightened his grip on Preacher's shoulder. "Don't go beating yourself up over this. When he put on the uniform, that soldier knew he was laying his life on the line, the same as you and I did the day we put on ours."

Preacher dragged an arm across his eyes. "Doesn't make it right."

"Wars are fought with only one rule in play. Kill or be killed."

Preacher set his jaw, his anger returning. "I hate this damn war. Hate what it does to people, the suffering it's caused, the lives it's taken."

Pops tightened his arm around Preacher and turned him away from the sight of the dead Vietcong. "This war's no different from any of those fought before it. It'll be the same for those yet to be fought."

Preacher jerked to stop, dragging Pops to a halt, as well. "How do you deal with it?" he cried in frustration. "How can you sleep at night, knowing people are dying all around you?"

"It's like I said before. I close my eyes and picture home. My wife, my son. It's them I'm fighting for, their safety, their freedom."

"And what happens when it's over? When you go home? Will you just forget everything you've seen, what you've done? Erase it all from your mind like it never happened?"

Pops shook his head sadly. "I don't know, Preacher. Right now all I can do is focus on making it home. The rest I'll worry about once I'm there."

He took the rifle Preacher still held. "You're a good man, Preacher. Of all the soldiers I've served with, you're the only one I can say with confidence will leave this godforsaken war with the same principles and standards he arrived with."

Preacher shook his head. "I don't feel like the same man. I feel…I don't know, scarred somehow."

Pops nodded grimly. "I read a quote somewhere. Can't remember who said it, but it went something like this. 'In war, there are no unwounded soldiers.' At the time I remember thinking the guy who said it must have been crazy. Now I think I understand what he meant."

"Yeah," Preacher said. "Me, too."

Squinting his eyes against the darkness, Pops looked off into the distance a long moment. "Preacher, I know you're going to find this hard to believe, but the soldiers who make it home are going to be burdened with a greater responsibility than the ones they've shouldered here."

Preacher looked at him in confusion. "How's that?"

His smile sad, Pops patted him on the back. "Focus on making it home, Preacher. When you get there, you'll know what I mean." Turning, he walked away. "You'll know, Preacher," he called over his shoulder. "You, of all people, will know."

One

Now, this is the life, Sally Gregg thought to herself. Swaying palm trees, a private pool, a house with every amenity known to man.

She tipped her sunglasses down and craned her neck to peer at the structure behind her. Not just a house, she corrected. It was a friggin' mansion. Nestled in Houston's prestigious River Oaks subdivision and situated on two lush acres, the house rivaled its neighbors in both design and size.

Too bad the interior doesn't reflect the traditional style of the exterior, she thought with regret. She supposed the ultramodern design suited her boss, but the mix of chrome and black lacquer didn't do a thing for her.

Thankfully her boss had limited the changes he'd

made after purchasing the house to the inside and had left the exterior and landscaping alone. As a result, the backyard was an oasis, as soothing to the soul as it was to the eye. A clever blend of French doors and floor-to-ceiling windows offered spectacular views of the pool and landscaped lawn beyond from inside the house.

Sure beats the heck out of the view of the parking lot from my apartment window, she thought with more than a little envy. With a sigh, she pushed her sunglasses back into place and settled on the lounge chair again.

But she'd have a house someday, she promised herself. Maybe not as large and grand as her boss's and definitely not one with a River Oaks address, but she'd have a home.

The only thing that kept her from having one now was money. Thanks to the generous salary her employer paid her and her own prudent lifestyle, she was steadily chipping away at that particular roadblock. Having learned frugality the hard way—by necessity—she knew how to stretch a dollar until it all but screamed for mercy. As a result she was close to becoming debt free, while still managing to squirrel away money toward a down payment.

Which she'd already have, if not for Brad.

She scowled at the reminder of her ex. She never should have given him the money, she thought bitterly. She, better than anyone, knew he'd never pay it back. Brad was, and always had been, fast with a promise and slow on delivery.

It was bad enough that she'd wasted four years of her

life with a man who didn't care for her, but then he'd decided to prolong her misery by showing up unannounced on her doorstep every time he needed money. For some stupid reason, he'd gotten it in his head that she owed him, which was insane, considering she had been the sole breadwinner throughout their marriage. Now she was forced to constantly move, in order to escape his mental abuse and the demands he made on her. As a result of the forced nomadic lifestyle, she had few possessions and even fewer friends.

She stubbornly pushed the thoughts of her ex from her mind. She wasn't letting Brad, or *anything*, for that matter, spoil her stay in paradise. And house-sitting for Vince Donnelly was exactly that. Paradise.

She shivered deliciously, thinking the stars definitely had been shining on her the day she'd snagged the job as Vince's executive secretary. Besides house-sitting for him when he was out of town—a perk she hadn't expected when she'd accepted the job—she received an above-average salary and more benefits than any of the other positions she'd applied for after moving to Houston. Granted, Vince wasn't the easiest man to work with. He was obsessive, demanding and micromanaged all of his employees. But he was also successful and drop-dead gorgeous.

Not that his looks had factored into her accepting the job as his secretary, she thought judiciously. Money was her motivator.

She remembered the shock she'd experienced when she'd walked into his office for her job interview and gotten her first look at the owner and founder of Donnelly Consulting. Based on the size and value of the company, she'd expected an older man. One with at least a spattering of gray at his temples.

What she'd found was a thirty-six-year-old hunk with the disposition of a grizzly bear.

With a shake of her head, she sat up and reached for the bottle of sunscreen, squirted a blob on her palm. Thirty minutes, she promised herself as she smoothed the cream over her arms, chest and legs, then she'd go inside and tackle the tasks her boss had e-mailed her overnight.

Grimacing, she mentally added *workaholic* to her boss's faults. The man was relentless. In the four months she'd worked for him, she'd never known him to take so much as a day off, which was a shame, since his business trips took him all over the world.

With a rueful shake of her head, she lay back and closed her eyes again. If *she* were required to take business trips all over the world, she'd darn well stay over a day or two and see the sights. Tokyo. Paris. Venice.

She smiled dreamily, easily able to imagine herself floating on a gondola along the canals of Venice.

"Sally!"

She shot up from the chair, to find her boss standing in the open French door.

"Vince," she said dully. Remembering how she was dressed, she snatched up a towel and whipped it around her. "What are you doing home? You aren't supposed to be back until Monday."

"Cut the trip short. Wasn't feeling good."

She peered at him more closely and had to admit he did look kind of sick. His face was pale, his shoulders stooped, his clothing rumpled. "Did you pick up a bug or something?"

Shaking his head, he rubbed a hand across his chest. "Heartburn. Something I ate must not have agreed with me."

She started toward him, praying whatever he had wasn't contagious. "When did you get sick?"

"Hit me last night. Caught a red-eye home." He braced a hand against the doorjamb as if needing its support as he turned inside the house. "Did you update the spreadsheets on the Holmes deal?"

She rolled her eyes, but dutifully followed him inside. "No."

He shot her a frown over his shoulder. "Didn't you get my e-mail?"

"Yes. This morning. I planned to do it this afternoon."

"I need that report *now*."

Before she could remind him it was Saturday and technically her day off, he clamped a hand over the back of a chair and bent double with a groan.

"Vince?" When he didn't reply, she moved around him to peer at his face and saw that his skin had turned a deathly gray and his breathing was labored. "Vince? Are you okay?"

He pressed a hand against his chest. "Can't breathe," he choked out.

She bolted for the kitchen, calling over her shoulder, "Stay right there. I'll get you a glass of water."

A step short of reaching her destination, she heard a loud crash behind her. Quickly reversing her direction, she raced back and found Vince sprawled on the floor and the stainless-steel end table that usually stood beside the chair on its side less than a foot from his head. She burned a full twenty seconds wringing her hands, trying to think what to do, then noticed his cell phone clipped at his waist. Snatching it from its holder, she punched in 911.

"911 operator. What is your emergency?"

She pressed a shaking hand to her forehead. "I'm not sure. I'm at my boss's house. He said he wasn't feeling well. I went to get him a glass a water. He must've fainted or something because now he's lying on the floor."

"Is he conscious?"

She shifted her gaze to Vince's closed eyes and gulped. "No."

"Your name?"

She frowned in confusion. "What?"

"Your name."

"Sally Gregg. Please," she begged. "Send an ambulance. I don't know what to do."

"Your relationship to the victim?"

"What difference does that make?" she cried. "The man needs help!"

"Try to remain calm, ma'am."

She drew in a deep breath and slowly released it, telling herself that losing her cool wasn't going to help things. "We're not related. He's my boss."

"The victim's name?"

"Vince Donnelly."

"Address?"

She rattled off Vince's address.

"Phone number?"

"For God's sake!" she snapped. "I don't want you to call me, I want an ambulance! He could be dying!"

"Ma'am, I understand your concern, but I'm required to collect this information."

"It's 555-423-6597," she said in a rush. "I'll leave the front door open."

Before the operator could ask her any more ridiculous questions, she threw down the phone and ran to unlock the front door, then raced back and dropped to a knee beside Vince.

"Vince? Vince, can you hear me?"

She held her breath, watching his face for a reaction and bit back a moan when not so much as an eyelash fluttered. "Vince, please," she begged. "Hold on. An ambulance is on the way."

There was a rap on the door.

"Houston Fire Department! Is there an emergency?"

Sally jumped to her feet. "In here!"

A man appeared, followed on his heels by a second man carrying a bag.

The first to arrive moved to stand with Sally, while the other dropped down beside Vince and began pulling equipment from his bag.

"What happened?" the man beside Sally asked.

She wrung her hands. "I don't know. He just returned from a trip. Said he wasn't feeling well. I went to get him a glass of water. He must have fainted, because I heard this loud crash. I ran back and found him lying on the floor."

"He's breathing," the second fireman reported.

A third man appeared and dropped down at Vince's head to support his neck while the second fireman fastened what looked like a thick, padded belt around it.

"What's he doing?" Sally asked in concern.

"Applying a C-collar," the man at her side explained. "In the event he injured his neck when he fell, the collar will prevent further damage."

Gulping, Sally watched as the men continued to work, one attaching a heart monitor to Vince's chest, the other wrapping a blood pressure cuff around his arm.

"EMS!"

Sally snapped up her head to see two more uniformed men rushing into the house, carrying a stretcher.

The man beside her quickly shifted his attention to the EMS team and reported, "Male, midthirties, possible cardiac arrest. Witness reports he passed out and hit his head on the table. We're holding C-spine, have applied oxygen via nonrebreather at fifteen liters per minute. Blood pressure 178/96, pulse is 102 respirations at 24 rapid."

Wide-eyed, Sally scooted out of the way and watched while the EMS team positioned a backboard beside Vince. On the count of three, the fireman rolled Vince to his side, and the EMS team slid the backboard into position. After lowering Vince to the backboard, they cinched straps around him to secure him. On the count of three again, the men lifted him onto the stretcher.

"You'll need to meet the ambulance at the hospital," the fireman told Sally, as the other men gathered their equipment, preparing to leave.

Sally took a step back. "Oh, I'm not family," she said. "I'm just his secretary."

The fireman gave her a slow look up and down and Sally cringed, knowing what he must think. A woman at her boss' house on the weekend wearing a towel wrapped around her? No, this didn't look good, at all.

The EMS team started toward the front door with Vince. The fireman placed a hand in the middle of Sally's back, urging her to follow.

He stopped on the porch. "Can you notify his family?"

"The only relative I know of is his mother, and she's confined to a nursing home."

"Then you'll need to go to the hospital."

"But I'm not family," she said again.

"Admittance is going to need whatever information you have to offer."

Leaving Sally on the porch, the fireman went to help the others load Vince into the back of the ambulance. One of the EMS team hopped into the back with Vince, while the other ran to climb behind the wheel of the vehicle. With lights flashing and siren screaming, the ambulance took off down the circle drive and bounced onto the street.

As Sally watched the vehicle disappear from sight, she sent up a silent prayer for Vince, then whispered another for her own forgiveness.

She might've prayed for Vince, but it was really her own welfare she was worried about.

If anything happened to her boss, she knew she'd be out of a job.

Sally spent the next eight hours in the hospital's emergency room. Upon her arrival, she'd provided the desk clerk with what information she could about Vince, which proved enough to allow them to locate his records, as well as his doctor. Technically, she could have left then, and with a clear conscious. But some weird sense of duty made her stay. Since she knew of no family or friends of Vince's to call to sit in her stead, she felt obligated to remain and await news of his condition.

During her long vigil, she read every magazine in the waiting room, drank four cups of coffee, made numerous trips to the restroom, one to the snack machine, and all without receiving any word on Vince's condition. Fearing the worst, she gathered her courage and approached the reception desk. The staff had changed at three o'clock, and a different woman now sat behind the desk, having replaced the clerk Sally had spoken to previously.

"Excuse me," she said, in order to get the clerk's attention. "Is there any word on Vince Donnelly?"

"Are you family?"

She shook her head. "His secretary."

"The doctor's still with Mr. Donnelly. I'll let him know you're here."

Sally murmured her thanks and returned to her seat. Desperate for something to help pass the time, she picked up a tattered paperback novel someone had left behind and began to read. As luck would have it, it was a mystery, her favorite genre, and two pages into the book, she was totally engrossed by the story.

"Are you Sally?"

She snapped up her head to find a doctor standing in front of her. Gulping, she set the book aside and slowly rose. "Y-yes. I'm Sally."

"I'm Dr. O'Connor, Vince's physician." He gestured toward a door. "If you'll come with me."

Sally followed him through the door and down a short hall.

Unsure what to expect, she asked uneasily, "He's going to be all right, isn't he?"

"That depends on Vince."

Considering that a nonanswer, she followed the doctor into one of the curtained-off examining rooms, where Vince lay, his eyes closed, his hands folded over the hospital gown that covered his chest. An IV tube ran from the back of one hand to a bottle hanging from a hook at the head of the bed. A white plastic bracelet circled his left wrist. She stared hard at his hands and breathed a sigh of relief when she saw the rhythmic rise and fall of his chest beneath them.

She sent up a silent prayer of thanks that he was still alive and her job hopefully secure, then whispered to the doctor, "Why hasn't he regained consciousness?"

"He did. His current state is drug induced."

At her questioning look, he went on to explain, "Vince doesn't make a very good patient. He regained consciousness shortly after arriving and pitched a fit when he realized where he was. I sedated him to calm him down."

Sally nodded, easily able to imagine the kind of ruckus her boss had kicked up. "Do you know what happened to him?"

"Before, during or after his fall?"

She shrugged. "All of it, I guess."

"He suffered a mild heart attack. The dizziness he experienced during the attack probably caused the fall. Unfortunately, on the way down he cracked his head on something and—"

"The end table," Sally interjected. "When I found him, the end table was lying next to him."

"Ah," the doctor said, nodding. "Stainless steel, as I recall. That explains the bump on the back of his head." He chuckled softly. "Too bad it didn't knock any sense into that thick skull of his."

Sally looked at the doctor curiously, surprised that he was familiar with Vince's home, as well as her boss's stubborn streak. "Do you know Vince?"

"Since we were kids." He glanced over at Vince and gave his head a rueful shake. "The most stubborn person I've ever had the misfortune to meet."

Sally would have laughed at the doctor's assessment of her boss, but she was too worried about her job to find anything amusing. "How long will he have to stay in the hospital?"

"I'd like to keep him a week, at the very least."

"Like hell you will."

Sally and the doctor both glanced over to find Vince awake and struggling to sit up.

The doctor quickly placed a hand against Vince's chest. "Unless you want me to put another knot on your head, I'd advise you to stay put."

Obviously too weak to put up much of a fight, Vince sank back against the pillow and squeezed his forehead between his fingers. "What'd you give me? I feel like I've been on a three-day drunk."

"It was a cocktail, all right, but not the kind you might expect."

Judging by Vince's weakened state, Sally had to believe whatever the doctor had given him was strong.

"I'm getting out of here."

The doctor looked down his nose at Vince. "You'll leave when I say you can."

Vince dropped his hand to scowl. "Don't be a jerk, Pat. You know I hate hospitals. Cut me loose so I can go home."

"You're in no condition to take care of yourself."

"I'll be fine as soon as the drugs wear off."

"You had a heart attack," the doctor reminded him. "Which is exactly what I've been telling you was going to happen if you didn't cut back on your workload and get rid of some of the stress in your life."

"There's nothing wrong with my heart," Vince grumbled.

"No, there's not," the doctor agreed. "Not this time, at least. The tests we ran indicated no damage was done to your heart. But you did suffer a concussion when you fell, which requires round-the-clock monitoring. Last I heard, you lived alone."

Vince glanced at Sally. She backed up a step, fearing she knew what he was going to suggest.

"Sally will take care of me."

She groaned inwardly.

The doctor turned to peer at her. "I thought the clerk said you were his secretary?"

"She is," Vince replied for her, then gave Sally a warning look. "And she can earn her salary at my house as easily as she can at my office."

The doctor kept his gaze fixed on Sally. "Would you seriously be willing to stay with this lug for a week?"

Sally stole a glance at Vince. The message in his eyes was clear: if she liked her job, she'd do as he said.

Turning back to the doctor, she forced a smile. "If that's what Vince wants."

"You'll be doing more than monitoring his sleep," the doctor warned her. "I've been telling him for years to slow down. This week he's going to do just that. No work. Period. And under no circumstances is he to leave the house. I want him resting, and when he's not resting, I want him relaxing and that means *no* phone calls and no e-mail. In fact, no contact with the outside world whatsoever. I don't want anything even remotely related to business anywhere near him. Got it?"

She nodded. "Yes, sir."

"And work on improving his nutrition. His eating habits are worse than a nine-year-old's."

"Yes, sir. I'll see that he eats properly balanced

meals. What about his physical activity? Should I monitor that, too?"

The doctor glanced at Vince, then shook his head. "No. In fact, it would probably do him some good, considering he spends most of his time sitting on an airplane or behind a desk."

"I'm sure I can think of something to keep him active."

The doctor studied her a long moment as if judging her ability to carry out his orders. "All right," he finally agreed, and headed out. "I'll write up instructions and sign his release."

As Sally watched the doctor disappear from sight, the enormity of the task she'd taken on sunk in. Panicking, she whipped her head around to level Vince with a threatening look. "Don't you move so much as a muscle. I'll be right back."

Flinging back the curtain, she ran after the doctor. "Dr. O'Connor! Wait!"

He glanced over his shoulder, then stopped and turned, a smile tugging at one corner of his mouth. "Changed your mind already?"

She dragged in a breath, choosing her words carefully, knowing she might very well be putting her job on the line. "I'm a secretary, not a nurse. I'm not sure I'm qualified to take care of someone who's had a heart attack. What if he should…" She swallowed hard, unable to voice her fears.

Chuckling, he shook his head. "Don't worry. Vince isn't going to die." He lifted a brow and added, "Though you might consider killing him before the week's over."

"But he had a heart attack," she said in frustration. "I'd think he'd need to stay in the hospital for at least a couple of days."

"Under normal circumstances, I'd keep him overnight." He shrugged. "But his attack was mild. More a warning, really. What he needs is rest and lots of it. Keeping him in the hospital, in Vince's case, would actually do him more harm than good."

Sally gave him a dubious look.

Chuckling, the doctor gave her shoulder a reassuring pat. "Trust me. He really is better off at home."

And home is exactly where Sally took Vince.

Thanks to another shot of Dr. O'Connor's wonder drug prior to leaving the hospital, he slept throughout the ride. Sally was grateful for the reprieve. It gave her time to get a grip on her anger with her boss for putting her in such an awkward position.

Heck, she didn't want to spend the week at his house! Not with him in residence. He was hard enough to get along with when he was well. She couldn't imagine what a forced convalescence would do to his already disagreeable personality.

She shot a scowl at the passenger seat where Vince slept, his head tipped back, his jaw slack, his lips parted. Spoiled brat, she thought resentfully. Using her job to coerce her into agreeing to act as his nursemaid. And if he thought he'd found himself a way to avoid following his doctor's orders, he had a new think coming. She intended to see that he followed them to the letter.

Before the week was over, he'd be begging Dr. O'Connor to admit him to the hospital.

She parked her car close to the front door and rounded the vehicle to help her patient out.

"Vince?" She gave his arm a none-too-gentle poke. "We're home."

He roused slightly. "Home?"

His slurred speech let her know the shot was still working.

"Yes, home." She took his arm and gave it a tug. "Come on. I'll help you inside."

It seemed to take him forever to unfold his long legs from the interior of her compact car. Her one regret was that he was too sedated to be aware of his surroundings. He'd really hate knowing he'd ridden in a six-year-old economy car, when he was accustomed to tooling around in a sporty and luxurious Lexus SC.

Pleased that she'd reduced her boss to slumming, she helped him to his feet. When he staggered a step, she quickly moved beneath his arm and locked an arm around his waist.

"Don't you dare fall," she warned. "If you do, I'm leaving you where you land."

He looked down at her, his mouth slanted in a lopsided grin. "Ah, come on, Sal. You wouldn't leave me out here all by myself."

"Don't bet on it," she muttered. Taking a firmer grip on his waist, she urged him into motion. "Now walk."

She halted him at the door, pressed her thumb against the security monitor, marveling anew at the high-tech system, while waiting for it to recognize her print. When the green light beamed, she shoved open the door and maneuvered him over the threshold.

He veered in the direction of his home office.

"Oh, no, you don't," she said, and bulldozed him down the long hall that led to the master bedroom. Once inside, she pointed him toward the king size bed and gave him a shove. He fell like a ton of bricks across its top. She quickly flipped back the covers, pulled off his shoes and socks. She frowned at his shirt and slacks, thinking he'd rest more comfortably without them.

"So, suffer," she grumbled. Cupping her hands at his heels, she lifted his legs and swung them onto the bed. Winded by the effort, she gave herself a moment to catch her breath, then reached to pull the covers over him.

She started to turn away, then stopped and leaned to place her face within inches of his. "Sleep well, Vince," she whispered evilly. "When you wake up, you're going to find yourself in hell."

Two

While Vince slept, Sally got busy. Determined to see that her boss followed the doctor's orders, she gathered every phone in the house, including his cell, and locked them, along with his laptop, in the trunk of her car. Using her own laptop to communicate with, she connected to the Internet site of the cable company that provided both his television and Internet service and had them temporarily disconnected—an easy feat, since her duties as his secretary gave her access to all his accounts and passwords. Next she visited the sites of the local newspaper and United States Postal Service and put a hold on his subscription and mail for the week.

Satisfied she'd done all she could to sever his ability to communicate with the outside world, she moved on to the kitchen. Since she frequently house-sat for Vince, she was fully aware of his fondness for junk food and wasted no time stuffing his nutrition-empty stash into garbage bags and hauling it all out to the street for the garbage collector to pick up. Thankfully she always brought her own groceries when she was required to stay at his house, and only hoped she had enough food left to feed them both, until she could make arrangements with the supermarket to have more delivered.

Having made the first step toward improving his nutrition, she focused her attention on possible means of escape, should he try to make a run for it. She collected his vehicle keys, as well as the spares he kept in the mud room, and locked them in the glove box of her car. She considered sneaking into his room and confiscating all his shoes, but opted to forgo that drastic measure until he proved himself a flight risk.

Flight risk? She smothered a laugh. She was definitely going to have to cut back on the number of *Law & Order* episodes she watched.

Taking her cell phone in hand again, she dialed Vince's land phone and cell phone numbers and had his calls forwarded to her cell. As a last precaution, she muted the ring on her phone and hid it in her makeup bag in the guest room. Sure that she'd done all that was humanly possible to ensure Vince followed his doctor's orders, she collapsed on the sofa, exhausted.

She'd barely closed her eyes, when she heard, "Sally!"

Groaning, she peeled herself from the couch and to

her feet. It appeared the bear had awakened from his drug-induced nap.

"Coming," she called wearily. When she reached his room, she found him sitting on the side of his bed, his clothes rumpled, his feet bare, his hair sticking up every which way. All-in-all, he looked like hell, which pleased her enormously.

She pasted on a cheerful smile. "Feeling better?"

He lifted his head to scowl at her. "Where the hell is my cell phone?"

To place herself out of harm's way, she picked up his shoes and socks and carried them to his closet, which was as large as her entire apartment. "Gone."

"What do you mean, *gone?*"

She slipped his shoes into an empty cubby and dropped his socks into the hamper. "Dr. O'Connor said you were to have no contact with the outside world."

"Screw what Pat said. I want my phone."

She opened her hands. "Sorry. Just following the doctor's orders."

He burned her with a look. "My doctor doesn't pay your salary. I do."

"I'm aware of that. But remember, this was your idea. You told Dr. O'Connor I could earn my salary at your house as easily as I could at your office. With the change in location, my duties changed, as well. For the time being I'm your caretaker, not your secretary, and I take my responsibilities very seriously."

"I don't need taking care of. What I need is my phone."

"Sorry. It's inaccessible for the week."

He leaped to his feet, his face flushed with anger. The quick movement must have made him light-headed, because the color drained from his face and he began to sway.

Fearing he was having another attack, Sally ran to grab his arm and urged him back to the edge of the bed. "Are you okay?"

"Moved too fast, is all."

She pressed a hand to her heart, then dropped it to fist at her side. "You really shouldn't upset yourself like that. You just had a heart attack. Do you want to bring on another?"

"There's nothing wrong with me," he grumbled.

She folded her arms across her chest and looked down her nose at him. "Oh, really? I could have sworn that Dr. O'Connor said you'd had a heart attack."

"That's how Pat earns his big fees. Makes up all kinds of ailments so his patients have to keep coming back to him."

Sally shook her head sadly. "You are so in denial."

He looked up to glare at her. "If I say there's nothing wrong with me, nothing is."

She turned away with a shrug. "Then there's no need for me to stay. I'll just give Dr. O'Connor a call and tell him I'm going home."

She made it as far as the door before he stopped her. "Wait."

She turned and lifted a brow in question.

"Don't call Pat. He'll come over."

"And that's a bad thing?"

"Damn right it is! He'll just drag me back to the hospital."

She wrinkled her nose in sympathy. "Probably."

Grimacing, he dragged a hand over his hair, then dropped it with a sigh to grip the edge of the bed. "I guess you'd better stay."

"I don't know," she said uncertainly. "My purpose in being here is to see that you follow your doctor's orders. If you aren't willing to cooperate, you really should be in the hospital where someone can look after you."

He paled at the mere suggestion. "I can't go back. I'll go crazy, if I do."

What little bit of patience she had for him snapped. "Oh, for heaven's sake, Vince. Don't be such a baby. There's nothing wrong with hospitals."

"Spend a month in one and try telling me that again."

Something in his voice told her he was speaking from experience. "You spent a month in a hospital?"

"Yeah. When I was a kid."

Curious to learn more, she crossed to the bed and sat down beside him. "Were you sick?"

He gave her a bland look. "No. I was on vacation."

She rolled her eyes. "Okay. Stupid question. So what was wrong with you?"

"Spinal meningitis. Spent a week at home in bed before the doctor admitted me. Another two weeks after he released me."

She stared, unable to imagine the severity of an illness that would require a child to remain bedridden for almost two months. "How old were you?"

"Nine. Missed two months of school. Had to drop out of the summer baseball program."

"Wow. That must have been tough."

"It sucked big-time."

"Were you left with any lasting effects?"

"Yeah," he said dryly. "I hate hospitals."

She hid a smile. "Yeah. I got that." She rose. "I'll bet you're hungry. When did you last eat?"

"I don't know. Sometime yesterday, I guess."

"I'll see what I can whip up."

He stood, too, though more slowly. "Have I got time to shower?"

She eyed him doubtfully. "Are you sure you're steady enough?"

"Positive."

She hesitated a moment longer, then turned away, deciding the alternative—bathing him herself—wasn't something she was willing to do.

"Fifteen minutes," she called to him.

After showering, Vince felt somewhat better and definitely more alert. He pulled on sweatpants and a T-shirt, keeping his movements slow to avoid another dizzy spell. Not that he was sick, he assured himself. He was healthy as a horse. He'd simply experienced a little…blip in his system. Nothing to be alarmed about, and certainly nothing that required hospitalization. He'd kick back for the remainder of the weekend, watch a little TV. By Monday he'd be as good as new and ready to get back to work.

Having resolved his health issues in his mind—and mentally conceded to a twenty-four-hour vacation to appease his doctor—he headed for the kitchen where he found Sally chopping vegetables at the island, dressed in, of all things, a bikini. He squeezed his eyes shut, sure that his mind was playing tricks on him, but when he opened them, her breasts were still pushing at the tiny electric-blue triangles that covered them. Beads of perspiration dotted the valley between her breasts. His mouth suddenly dry, he wet his lips and would swear he tasted salt and coconuts.

"Vince?"

He snapped his gaze to hers. He swallowed hard, then stole a quick look to confirm what she was wearing, and found the bikini was gone, replaced by shorts and a top. Wondering if the bump on his head had done more damage than he first thought, he asked hesitantly, "Did you change clothes?"

She looked at him curiously. "Well, yeah. While you were in the shower. Is that a problem?"

He gulped again, not wanting to ask but needing to know. "Do you own a blue bikini?"

Her eyes narrowed to slits.

He held up a hand. "Just answer the question. Do you own a blue bikini?"

"You know very well I do, since I was wearing it this morning when you arrived home."

He sagged his shoulders in relief. Thank God. He wasn't going crazy. A little addled maybe, but he wasn't delusional.

She slammed the knife to the counter. "Would you mind telling me what this is all about?"

"I...I was testing to see if the fall had affected my memory."

Though he could tell she didn't buy his story, thankfully she didn't question him further and began to chop again.

"I thought we'd eat on the patio," she said. "It's nice out."

He glanced at the wall of doors that opened to the patio and saw that she'd already set the table outside. A candle flickered in a lantern on its center. Although he preferred to eat his meals in front of the television, he decided it best to be agreeable—for the time being, anyway. "Whatever."

"What do you want to drink?"

"Beer," he said, and headed for the refrigerator to get it himself.

She put out a hand to stop him. "No alcoholic beverages."

"Why not?"

She tapped a finger against her head. "Concussion, remember? No alcohol for at least forty-eight hours."

He hitched his hands on his hips. "Says who?"

She pointed at a sheaf of papers lying on the corner of the island. "Doctor's orders."

He opened his mouth to tell her what she could do with his doctor's orders, then clamped it shut.

"Doctor's orders, my ass," he muttered under his breath, as he headed outside. Okay, so he'd play their little game for a while, but then he was done. First thing Monday morning it was business as usual for Vince Donnelly.

his hand and dumped the tablet on his palm.
All I know is you're to take one every night.
ers."

w, I'm a little sick of hearing that phrase."
ged and sat opposite him again. "You're
ng to be sicker of hearing it by the end of

, he popped the pill in his mouth, chased it
ater. He shuddered at the bitter aftertaste
mouth. "Satisfied?"
d. "For now."

ne Vince finished his second helping of
lids were heavy, his movements sluggish.
dn't know what was in the pill she'd given
atever it was, it obviously had the same
t as the shots his doctor had given him at

ed for his plate. "Tired?"

yawn, she rose. "Me, too. It's past ten.
ould call it a night."
pushed awkwardly to his feet.
s unsteadiness, she set down their plates.
ered, and moved next to him. "Lean on me."
d an arm over her shoulders and half
stumbled his way into the house. "Head's
l, his words slurring a bit.
k a smile, she guided him to his room.
red."

"Here you go," Sally said and slid a plate in front of him.

He looked down at the mountain of greens, then up at her. "What's this?"

She sat opposite him and draped her napkin over her lap. "Baby spinach, broccoli florets, julienne red peppers with some grilled salmon tossed in. The dressing is my own concoction. Balsamic vinegar, virgin olive oil and a few spices."

He shoved the plate away. "I hate salad."

With a shrug, she popped a forkful of greens into her mouth. "That's too bad, because that's all there is to eat."

Setting his jaw, he scraped back his chair and headed for the kitchen. He opened the pantry, the refrigerator, the freezer then stomped back to the door. "What the hell happened to all my food?"

She dabbed her mouth. "I threw it away."

"You *what?*"

"My instructions included seeing that you ate nutritional meals." She smiled and lifted her fork. "You really should try this. It's pretty darn tasty, even if I do say so myself."

Vince dropped his head back, in a silent plea for mercy. A weekend, he reminded himself. Less, since technically the weekend was half-over. His stomach chose that moment to growl, reminding him how long it had been since he'd eaten.

Scowling, he stomped back to the table and snatched his plate in front of him again. With his nose curled in disgust, he stabbed a spinach leaf and poked it into his mouth, chewed. His taste buds exploded, registering the tart, smoky flavor of the balsamic vinegar and the unfamiliar spices in the dressing. He forced himself to swallow, then waited, half expecting the food to come right back up. When it didn't, he scooped up another bite, shoveled it into his mouth.

"Listen to that."

He glanced up to find Sally staring off into the distance, her lips curved in a soft smile. He looked around. "What? I don't hear anything."

She patted the air to silence him. "Just listen."

He scooped up more salad and listened while he chewed. "I still don't hear anything."

"Probably because you're accustomed to hearing it. Water tumbling over stone, the rustle of wind through the trees. Nature's own symphony."

He cocked his head and listened a moment, then resumed eating. "If you say so."

"Some people find the sounds of nature relaxing. In fact, there's an entire section dedicated to it in music stores."

He glanced up to see if she was pulling his leg. "Seriously?"

Hiding a smile, she sipped her water. "Obviously you've never had a massage."

"What does a massage have to do with anything?"

"Sounds from nature are a staple at spas. Masseuses play them in the background when giving massages."

With a shrug he attacked his salad again. "Learn something new every day."

"What kind of music do you listen to?"

Once his bed was in sight, he dropped his arm from around her and started for it, stripping his shirt over his head. When he pushed at the waist of his sweatpants, she clamped her eyes shut, not sure what he was wearing beneath them. She waited until she heard the soft *whoosh* of the mattress accepting his weight and the rustle of bedcovers, before stealing a peek. Relieved to find he'd pulled the covers to his waist and was decently covered, she walked to the bed.

Placing a hand on the edge of the mattress for balance, she leaned to switch off the wall lamp above his head. Just as the light winked out, a weight fell over her hand. She glanced down to find his hand covered hers, then snapped her gaze to his. Though it was dark, there was enough natural illumination for her to see that he was looking at her. His lids were heavy and his shuttered eyes were stained the rich brown of freshly brewed coffee. In them she saw a vulnerability she was unaccustomed to seeing in her boss's eyes.

"Stay."

The request was one-word simple and would've been easy for her to refuse, if not for the plea she heard in it. She hesitated, wanting nothing more than a good night's sleep after the long, stress-filled day she'd put in.

"I'll be checking on you through the night," she assured him. "If you need me, all you have to do is call."

She started to ease her hand from beneath his, but he closed his fingers around hers.

"What if I…can't?"

The possibility sent a chill down her spine and her

reaching behind her to drag a chair close to the bed. "Okay. I'll stay."

The tension in his grasp relaxed a bit, but his fingers remained curled around hers. Watching him closely, she knew, by the smoothing of his features, the instant sleep took him.

With nothing else to do, she continued to study him. She'd always considered her boss handsome, but slumber added a new quality for her to consider. It softened his features, making him look younger and much less forbidding than he did when awake. Remembering the story he'd told her about his childhood illness, she squinted her eyes and tried to imagine what he'd looked like as a boy. She smothered a laugh, pitying the nurses who were required to care for him there. It was easy enough to picture a child-size, miniature version of him, griping about the hospital food and driving his parents crazy with his demands.

Her amusement slowly faded as she wondered if it was his parents who were responsible for shaping his personality.

What was it her grandmother used to say? *Teach a child to laugh and he'll carry that gift with him throughout life.*

Her grandmother was by no means an authority on child rearing, but after teaching school for thirty years and raising two children of her own, plus Sally after Sally's mother's death, she had enough experience to fill a book on the subject.

Sally frowned thoughtfully, trying to remember if she'd ever heard Vince laugh, and couldn't come up

"Here you go," Sally said and slid a plate in front of him.

He looked down at the mountain of greens, then up at her. "What's this?"

She sat opposite him and draped her napkin over her lap. "Baby spinach, broccoli florets, julienne red peppers with some grilled salmon tossed in. The dressing is my own concoction. Balsamic vinegar, virgin olive oil and a few spices."

He shoved the plate away. "I hate salad."

With a shrug, she popped a forkful of greens into her mouth. "That's too bad, because that's all there is to eat."

Setting his jaw, he scraped back his chair and headed for the kitchen. He opened the pantry, the refrigerator, the freezer then stomped back to the door. "What the hell happened to all my food?"

She dabbed her mouth. "I threw it away."

"You *what?*"

"My instructions included seeing that you ate nutritional meals." She smiled and lifted her fork. "You really should try this. It's pretty darn tasty, even if I do say so myself."

Vince dropped his head back, in a silent plea for mercy. A weekend, he reminded himself. Less, since technically the weekend was half-over. His stomach chose that moment to growl, reminding him how long it had been since he'd eaten.

Scowling, he stomped back to the table and snatched his plate in front of him again. With his nose curled in disgust, he stabbed a spinach leaf and poked it into his mouth, chewed. His taste buds exploded, registering the tart, smoky flavor of the balsamic vinegar and the unfamiliar spices in the dressing. He forced himself to swallow, then waited, half expecting the food to come right back up. When it didn't, he scooped up another bite, shoveled it into his mouth.

"Listen to that."

He glanced up to find Sally staring off into the distance, her lips curved in a soft smile. He looked around. "What? I don't hear anything."

She patted the air to silence him. "Just listen."

He scooped up more salad and listened while he chewed. "I still don't hear anything."

"Probably because you're accustomed to hearing it. Water tumbling over stone, the rustle of wind through the trees. Nature's own symphony."

He cocked his head and listened a moment, then resumed eating. "If you say so."

"Some people find the sounds of nature relaxing. In fact, there's an entire section dedicated to it in music stores."

He glanced up to see if she was pulling his leg. "Seriously?"

Hiding a smile, she sipped her water. "Obviously you've never had a massage."

"What does a massage have to do with anything?"

"Sounds from nature are a staple at spas. Masseuses play them in the background when giving massages."

With a shrug he attacked his salad again. "Learn something new every day."

"What kind of music do you listen to?"

He considered a moment, then shook his head. "I don't."

"Don't you ever turn the radio on in your car?"

"Yeah, to the stock report."

"You really should try tuning to a music station."

"Why?"

"Well, for one thing it's soothing."

He snorted a laugh. "You must like that longhair stuff."

"Sometimes. Depends on my mood or the situation. I prefer rock when I'm cleaning house. Keeps me moving."

"I'll suggest that to my housekeeper."

"How's your head?"

He reached for the bottle of water she'd set by his plate. "Fine."

"No headache?"

"Nope."

"How's your vision?"

"Twenty-twenty."

She rolled her eyes. "I meant, is it blurry?"

He blinked hard and opened his eyes wide, as if to test them. "Nope," he reported. "Clear as a bell."

"Would you like some more salad?"

He looked down and was surprised to see that he'd eaten every bite. He handed her his plate. "Why not?"

She set aside her napkin and rose.

"And put some more of that salmon on it," he called after her. "That stuff's not half-bad."

When she returned, she set the plate in front of him, then opened her hand. Vince eyed the pill nesting on her palm. "What's that?"

She took his hand and dumped the tablet on his palm. "Beats me. All I know is you're to take one every night. Doctor's orders."

"You know, I'm a little sick of hearing that phrase."

She shrugged and sat opposite him again. "You're probably going to be sicker of hearing it by the end of the week."

Scowling, he popped the pill in his mouth, chased it down with water. He shuddered at the bitter aftertaste it left in his mouth. "Satisfied?"

She smiled. "For now."

By the time Vince finished his second helping of salad, his eyelids were heavy, his movements sluggish. Sally truly didn't know what was in the pill she'd given him, but whatever it was, it obviously had the same sedative effect as the shots his doctor had given him at the hospital.

She reached for his plate. "Tired?"

"A little."

Stifling a yawn, she rose. "Me, too. It's past ten. Maybe we should call it a night."

"Yeah." He pushed awkwardly to his feet.

Noticing his unsteadiness, she set down their plates. "Here," she offered, and moved next to him. "Lean on me."

He dropped an arm over her shoulders and half shuffled, half stumbled his way into the house. "Head's fuzzy," he said, his words slurring a bit.

Biting back a smile, she guided him to his room. "You're just tired."

with a single instance. Smile, maybe, but never an out-and-out laugh. Were his parents that way, too? If so, it would certainly explain his sour attitude.

Since she had no way of knowing who or what had shaped Vince, she pushed the troublesome thoughts aside and focused on his face again.

It wasn't a chore, as he was easy to look at. His features were undeniably masculine—square jaw, high slash of cheekbone, and his whiskey-colored eyes, when open, were sharp, hinting at a keen mind. His mouth, in sleep, was soft, his lower lip fuller than the upper, which was a total contradiction to the impatience that shaped them when he was awake.

She shook her head sadly, thinking it was a shame such a sexy mouth was wasted on a man with such an unappealing demeanor. As she studied his mouth, her mind drifted, imagining what those lips would feel like pressed against hers. The texture, the pressure. His taste.

She reached to touch a finger to his lips, but caught herself in the nick of time and snatched her hand back to hold against her waist. Mortified by her carnal thoughts, she forced her gaze from his face and to the abstract painting on the far wall.

The painting, like everything else in Vince's house, was devoid of color, of life. Angry slashes of gray, taupe and black streaked the canvas. It was an original and had cost Vince over a hundred thousand dollars—Sally knew, because she was the one who had contacted his insurance company to have them add the value to his homeowner's policy. But in her opinion, it was hideous…and exactly the distraction she needed to keep her mind off Vince and his oh-so-kissable mouth.

As she stared at the ugly painting, her eyelids grew heavy, her head heavier still. Her chin dropped to her chest and she snapped it up, blinking rapidly to force herself awake. Afraid she'd fall asleep and not wake Vince during the night as the doctor had instructed, she eased her hand from beneath his and tiptoed to her room for her alarm clock. After setting it for midnight, she placed it on the bedside table, then settled on the chair again. Within seconds her eyelids drooped.

This time she allowed herself to sleep.

Promptly at midnight the alarm went off, jarring Sally awake. Bleary-eyed, she groped to switch it off, then stood to stretch the kinks from her back.

"Vince?" she called softly. When he didn't respond, she said a little louder, "Vince."

His eyelids shot up, then slowly drifted down.

Smothering a laugh, she shook his shoulder. "Vince, wake up."

Moaning, he pulled the pillow over his head.

She hesitated a moment, unsure how much of a reaction she should expect from a concussion victim. Deciding coherency was necessary, she poked his shoulder. "Vince? I need you to talk to me."

He mumbled something unintelligible, and she lifted the pillow from his head. "What did you say?"

His arm snaked out and hooked around her neck. Before she could react, she found herself lying face-to-face with him. She kicked, trying to break free, but he tossed a leg over hers, pinning them down.

"Vince!" she cried.

He rolled on top of her and pressed his mouth to hers. "Shh. Later. Gotta recoup."

Recoup? What the heck was he talking about?

Her eyes bugged, as she realized he must think she wanted to have sex with him. She struggled against him, but found she was trapped by his weight.

"Vince. Vince!"

His only response was a snore.

She pushed at his chest in frustration, but gained not so much as an inch.

"Great," she muttered irritably. She lay there a moment trying to think what to do, but quickly concluded there was nothing she *could* do.

Until he moved on his own or the sedative wore off, it appeared she was stuck right were she was.

As Vince's human teddy bear.

Yawning, Sally opened her eyes, but froze when she found Vince's face opposite hers. At some point in the night, he must have moved, because she was no longer trapped beneath him, but was lying on her side facing him. One of his arms draped her waist, the other pillowed her head.

Praying she could slip out of bed before he awakened, she caught his arm between thumb and finger and gingerly lifted it from her waist. He snuffled once, but his eyes remained blessedly closed. Keeping her gaze fixed on his face, she eased from the bed and reached for her alarm clock, planning to make a fast exit.

Just as her fingers closed over the clock, his eyelids flipped open.

She pasted on a bright smile. "Good morning. Did you sleep well?"

He peered at her a long moment, his forehead creasing in confusion, then dragged himself up to a sitting position and rubbed a hand over his hair. "Yeah. I think so." Frowning, he glanced at the empty space beside him, then slanted her a look. "Did you?"

Oh, God, she thought in horror. He knew! In spite of his drugged state, somehow he must know she'd slept with him.

Though it was difficult, she managed to keep her smile in place and hopefully the mortification from her expression. "Fine. Just fine."

Clutching her alarm clock to her chest, she all but ran for the door. "I'm going to take a quick shower," she called over her shoulder. "Afterward, I'll start breakfast."

Three

While she sliced fruit for breakfast, Sally tried not to think about the moment she would have to face Vince. It was just so humiliating, him knowing she'd slept in the same bed with him. But judging by the suspicious way he'd looked at her, she had to believe he not only knew but thought it had been her idea, which was totally unfair, considering *he* was the one who had put her there.

Scowling, she set the knife down and went to the refrigerator for the yogurt she intended to mix with the fruit. When she turned, she stopped short. Vince stood in the doorway watching her, his shoulder braced against the jamb. Khaki shorts rode low on his waist, his chest was bare. Realizing she was staring, she dropped her gaze and continued on to the island.

"If you wanted to sleep with me, you had only to ask."

She snapped up her head, then dropped it, her cheeks flaming. "It wasn't like I wanted to," she groused, as she dumped the yogurt over the fruit.

"Really? Then why did you?"

Furious that he seemed intent on blaming her for something totally out of her control, she snatched up a spoon, stirred. "You left me little choice."

"Me? Last thing I remember, I was in bed alone."

She whacked the spoon against the side of the bowl and wished it was his head. "I tried to wake you. You grabbed me, dragged me into bed. That's how it happened. Period."

"And since you were comfortable, you decided to stay."

She snorted. "Believe me. I was anything but comfortable."

He crossed to the island, took the spoon from her and dipped it into the fruit mixture. "Then why didn't you leave?"

"Because you were on top of me! I could barely breathe, much less move."

He gave her a chiding look as he brought the spoon to his mouth. "Do you really expect me to believe that?"

Fearing she'd kill him if she remained in the room another minute, she spun away. "Believe whatever you want."

"Where are you going?" he called after her.

"To my room."

"The one you slept in last night? Or the one across the hall from mine?"

She slowed, then marched on, her hands doubled into fists at her sides.

"Sally!"

She drew in a deep breath and snapped, "What?"

"The TV won't work."

Groaning, she did a reluctant about-face, knowing full well she and Captain Friendly were about to go another round.

She found him in the den, holding the remote aimed at the TV. On the screen was nothing but snow. She watched him punch the power button, punch it again.

"Problem?" she asked innocently.

"There's no reception." He crossed to the unit and checked the cable connections, then shot her an accusing look over his shoulder. "You did something to it, didn't you?"

She opened her hands. "Doctor's orders."

He straightened, a vein bulging on his temple. "Pat didn't say anything about me watching TV."

"'No contact with the outside world,'" she said, quoting the doctor. "Television falls into that category."

He glared at her, smoke all but coming out his ears, then drew his arm back, as if he intended to throw the remote at her. Refusing to be intimidated, she jutted her chin.

His arm hung suspended a moment, then he brought it down hard. The remote cracked against the granite tiles and exploded, sending shards of black plastic flying and batteries rolling crazily across the room.

She made a tsking sound with her tongue. "You

know, I'd expect that kind of behavior from a two-year-old, but certainly not a grown man."

Curling his lip in a snarl, he spun and stalked away.

Sally didn't return to her room. She didn't have to, since Vince had holed up in his.

He remained there the remainder of the morning and part of the afternoon. She would've worried when he didn't surface for lunch, but disposed of her concerns by reminding herself that he was an adult and knew where to find food if he was hungry.

Determined not to allow him to spoil her day any more than he already had, after eating her own lunch she changed into her swimsuit, grabbed the paperback she had brought with her from the emergency room and headed for the pool.

She'd read two chapters when she heard the patio door open behind her. She knew it was Vince, but didn't feel the need to acknowledge his presence, since he hadn't bothered to acknowledge hers.

She listened to the pad of his footsteps on the patio's stone floor, but continued to read.

He cleared his throat, and she stubbornly kept her gaze on the page, determined to make him speak first.

His shadow fell over her and the book was snatched from her hands.

She tipped her sunglasses down to glare at him. "Excuse me, but I was reading that."

"I'm bored."

She plucked the book from his hand. "So find your own book to read. This one's mine."

Instead of leaving as she'd hoped he would, he flopped down on the edge of the lounge chair.

"I'm tired of reading."

She stole a peek at him over the top of her book and saw that he really did look miserable. His shoulders were slumped, his expression hang-dog sad. Reminding herself that it was her job to care for him—for the week, anyway—with a sigh, she set aside her book. "Okay, so what do you want to do?"

"No TV, no phone, no computer. What's left?"

Spoiled brat, she thought peevishly. Take away his toys and he's at a loss as to how to entertain himself. Pulling off her sunglasses, she hooked them over the arm of her chair. "How about a swim?"

He glanced at the pool, as if he'd forgotten it was there, until she'd mentioned it. "What's so great about swimming?"

She looked at him in disbelief. "Are you telling me you have a pool and you never use it?"

He lifted a shoulder. "It was here when I bought the place."

With a rueful shake of her head, she rose from the lounge chair. "Come on, Tarzan. Jane will introduce you to the pleasures of pool ownership."

She crossed to the edge and dipped a foot into the water. "Is it cold?"

She glanced over to find he had joined her and was eyeing the water warily. "Cool, but pleasantly so."

He drew back. "I don't have on a suit."

She glanced down and saw that he was wearing the same shorts he'd had on that morning. "What you have on will do." When he continued to hang back, she decided a challenge might get him in the water. "Last one to reach the opposite side has to do the dinner dishes," she dared, then dived in.

The water *was* cold, she thought with a shiver, as it streamed along her sun-warmed skin. But it felt marvelous. Surfacing, she began to swim but was careful to keep her strokes slow. If Vince had accepted her challenge and followed her in, she didn't think it wise to humiliate him by beating him by too large a margin.

Just as her fingers brushed the wall, a weight pressed on her head and pushed her under. She came up sputtering and scraping back her hair to find Vince lounging opposite her, his arms stretched along the edge of the pool, his hair dripping water.

She glanced over her shoulder at the house and the spot where she'd left him, then back at him. "You beat me?" she asked incredulously.

"By at least three strokes. Looks like you're going to be doing the dishes tonight."

She flattened her lips. "I wouldn't be, if I'd known it was a real race."

"You were the one who offered the challenge."

"Yeah, but I wasn't sure you could swim, so I held back."

With a shrug, he pushed off from the side and rolled to his back, stroking his arms in a lazy backstroke. "Doesn't change the results. You're still doing the dishes."

"As if you would've done them, anyway," she grumbled under her breath.

He cupped a hand at his ear. "Is that sour grapes I hear?"

She swam to catch up with him. "Has anyone ever told you it's unsportsmanlike to gloat?"

"Whining doesn't change the results."

She drew even with him and rolled to her back, matching him stroke for stroke. "I'm not whining."

"Sounds like it to me."

Irritated that he seemed determined to rub her nose in her loss, she pushed her feet down to stand chin deep in the water. "All right, already! You won. So get over it."

Closing his eyes, he stretched out his arms and let himself float. "Glad you were finally able to face the ugly truth."

She wanted to slug him. Considered drowning him. But ended up laughing instead. "Your ego is downright scary."

"Nothing wrong with my ego."

"Nothing but its size."

His only response was a smug smile.

She shook her head ruefully, finding it difficult to associate this man with the one she knew as her boss. He looked so relaxed floating there, his eyes closed, his body limp as a rag. Nothing at all like the micromanaging, nitpicking tyrant she knew from the office.

Her gaze settled on his chest and her thoughts slipped to the previous night. She remembered the shock she'd felt when he'd hooked his arm around her neck and dragged her down, the panic that had seized her when she'd realized she was trapped beneath him. She remembered the weight of his body on hers, her breasts flattened beneath his chest, his legs twined with her.

What was more, she had a fleeting memory of being held in his arms, his body no longer weighing on her, but stretched alongside, her cheek nestled against his chest. As the memory built, she could almost hear the rhythmic beat of his heart, feel the slow stroke of his hand over her hair, down her back.

She gulped, staring at the beads of water gleaming on his chest and wondered if she'd dreamed that last part or if it had really happened.

Her gaze slid to his mouth.

He'd kissed her.

Not a real kiss, she reminded herself. Not the passionate kind, at any rate. It had lasted no more than a second or two. But she remembered the pressure of his mouth on hers, the whisper of his breath against her lips when he'd shushed her, and wondered what it would feel like if he were to *really* kiss her.

"Sally?"

She jumped, then snapped her gaze to his and found him looking at her. "S-sorry. Did you say something?"

A slow, knowing smile curved his lips. "Yeah, but I bet it wasn't nearly as interesting as what you were thinking."

Heat flamed in her cheeks. "I—I wasn't thinking anything."

His smile widening, he stood, sending water to lap

against her chest. "Yeah, you were. You were thinking about last night."

Shaking her head, she backed up a step. "No. Really. My mind was blank. Empty."

He started toward her, using his hands to push his way through the water. "Liar."

Her back hit the side of the pool and she thrust out a hand. "You're being ridiculous, and I want you to stop right now."

He brushed her hand aside and moved in close. So close she had to tip her head back to look at him.

"Are you sure?" he asked.

"Yes!" She gave his chest an impatient shove, but she might as well have saved her strength, because it was like trying to move a brick wall.

"Liar."

She sucked in an indignant breath.

"Don't try denying it," he warned. "Part of my success is due to my ability to read people. Right now you're embarrassed or, at the very least, flustered."

Because she was both, she clamped her jaw down, fearing any attempt on her part to disavow his claim would only prove him right.

"A moment ago you were looking at my mouth," he went on. "Your cheeks were red then, too, because you were thinking about kissing me."

Flattening her lips, she turned her face away. "You really should do something about that ego of yours."

"Desire and embarrassment produce similar reactions. Flushed cheeks."

She angled her head to narrow an eye at him. "I'm in the sun. It's hot. My face always turns red when I'm hot."

He placed a finger beneath her chin and forced her face to his. "There's a difference between heat produced from within and that produced by external forces. It stains the skin differently." He swept a knuckle along the ridge of her cheekbone. "When you were looking at my mouth, that was definitely lust."

Hypnotized by the satiny stroke of his finger, it took a moment for what he said to register. When it did, she slapped at his hand. "If you're through analyzing me, I'd appreciate it if you would move. I'd like to get out of the pool before I turn into a prune."

Instead of giving her the room she'd requested, he edged closer. "I don't remember much about last night. It's those damn pills. They really knock me on my butt." He angled his head to peer at her curiously. "Did we kiss?"

"We certainly did not," she said indignantly. "You shushed me, is all."

"With my mouth?"

"Yes!"

"Was it good?"

She tossed up her hands. "How would I know? It happened too fast for me to know whether it was good or not."

He nodded. "That explains it, then."

"Explains, *what?*"

"What you were thinking about earlier when you were looking at my mouth. You were wondering what it be like to kiss me."

Scowling, she turned her face away. "Yeah, right."

"Let's find out."

Panicking, she whipped her face back to his. "Are you crazy? I don't want to kiss you! I—"

His mouth slammed down over hers, smothering her refusal. She kicked and pushed at him, trying to break free, but he merely vised his arms around her and pressed her back against the side of the pool, making escape impossible. Determined to remain unaffected, she kept her lips pressed tightly together and mentally recited the grocery list she'd made while eating lunch.

Skim milk.

Whole wheat bread.

His hands slid down her back to cup her buttocks.

She squeezed her eyes shut, trying to visualize the third item on the list, so she wouldn't think about his hands and how strong they felt or the delicious sensations they stirred inside her.

Bagels! Yes, bagels!

His fingers kneaded.

Though she struggled to keep her mind diverted, her body instinctively arched against him, a move that proved disastrous. One prod of his erection against her abdomen, and the grocery list blinked from her mind. A moan vibrated low in her throat, rose to slide past her slightly parted lips.

Taking advantage of the lapse in her guard, he used his tongue to widen the gap, then slipped it inside. Her knees went weak as his tongue swept over hers, her mind turned to dust. She knew she should make him stop, push him away…but she couldn't. She was too immersed in sensation to do anything but let herself be swept along for the ride.

And, oh, what a ride it was.

His hands caressed her buttocks, her back, then lifted to frame her face, while he continued to plunder her mouth with his tongue. She felt the pressure of his thumbs at her jaw, holding her face up to his; nearly wept at the slow, sensual roll of his hips against her groin. Of their own accord, her arms lifted to wind around his neck, her fingers to fist in his hair. When that connection proved inadequate, she wrapped a leg around his thighs and drew his hips closer.

Every part of his body moved in sync with his tongue in a dance bent on seduction. Heat rushed through her veins, gathered to swirl low in her abdomen. She hadn't been kissed like this in more than four years, even longer since she'd experienced this strong a need. Yet she recognized it for what it was. Lust.

That he'd succeeded in proving that she wanted to kiss him didn't matter. Not any longer. All she could think was *more*.

"Sally?"

It took her a moment to realize that his mouth was no longer on hers. Another to find the strength to open her eyes.

"Want to try telling me that again?"

She opened her mouth to lie a second time, but the words wouldn't come.

His smile smug, he heaved himself up onto the pool deck. "That's what I thought."

This time it was Sally who holed up in her room.

After showering and changing, she flopped down on her bed, sure that she'd never find the courage to step beyond the bedroom door again. She was mortified. Humiliated! She couldn't face Vince now. Not after all but melting at his feet in a puddle of need.

Sickened by her weakness, furious with him for exposing it, she buried her face in her hands. "What am I going to do?" she moaned miserably. She couldn't stay in his house any longer. She wasn't even sure she could continue to work for him. Seeing him at the office every day would simply be too humiliating, too embarrassing to endure. Her coworkers would find out. Somehow they always seemed to know everything. No one, not even the boss, was safe from office gossip. They would whisper behind her back, laugh at her gullibility, her stupidity.

She dropped her hands to fist in her lap, resentment bubbling up inside her at the injustice of it all. He'd played her for a fool. Toyed with her. Put her job, her reputation, in jeopardy! He'd probably staged the entire thing, thinking she'd run home with her tail tucked between her legs and he would be free to ignore his doctor's orders.

She pushed off the bed. Well, if he thought he could rid himself of her so easily, he had another think coming. She wasn't running anywhere, not even as far as the guest room. She was a mature woman. She knew how to handle adversity. Hadn't she stayed married to an egomaniac for four years? A man who thought only of himself, never once considering the wants or needs of others, not even his own wife's? Facing Vince Donnelly would be a piece of cake, compared to the agony and humiliation her ex had put her through, both during and after their marriage.

She began to pace, trying to think how best to handle the situation. As far as she could see, she had three choices. One, she could pack up and go home and leave Vince to take care of himself. Two, she could admit ownership for her active participation in the kiss, blame her weakness on the effects of sitting in the sun too long and let him know in no uncertain terms that it wouldn't happen again. Or, three, she could pretend the kiss had never happened.

The first was the most tempting, but she'd already decided she wasn't running away.

The second held merit, but the mere thought of admitting that his kiss had melted her bones left a bitter taste in her mouth. Having to witness his smugness, suffer his overinflated ego… She shuddered. She simply couldn't do it.

Which left pretending the kiss had never happened.

Confident that she could pull off the charade, she went to the kitchen to prepare dinner and was relieved when she didn't bump into Vince along the way. Since her food supplies were quickly dwindling, she set out what items remained. Three tomatoes, a package of fresh basil, a couple of eggs, a half loaf of French bread, less than a quart of milk, a container of yogurt. She studied them thoughtfully, trying to think what she could prepare that would be nutritious, yet something Vince wouldn't curl up his nose at.

Tomato-basil Soup?

Keeping her fingers crossed that she'd find the missing ingredient she needed to prepare the dish, she dug around in the pantry until she unearthed two cans of broth.

Considering Vince's food preferences, she had to believe the broth was hers and left behind from a previous house-sitting commitment. With all the tools needed now at hand, she began cutting up the vegetables and herbs and dropping them into a saucepan to simmer in olive oil. While the vegetables cooked, she sliced what remained of the loaf of French bread and spread it with garlic butter. She placed the slices on a baking sheet, then sprinkled the tops with Parmesan cheese and popped the bread into the oven to bake. Returning to the stove, she stirred the tomatoes and basil, her mouth watering at the fragrant aromas that rose from the pan.

Arms circled her waist from behind and she tensed, knowing it was Vince. Before she could move, he dipped his head to nuzzle her neck.

"Something sure smells good."

Remembering her decision to pretend the kiss had never happened, she carefully eased from his embrace and moved to the oven to check the bread. "Tomato-basil soup. It was the only thing I could think to make with the ingredients I have left."

He trailed her to the oven and succeeded in blocking her in. "What's that?"

With his body pressed at her back, a heat rivaling that wafting from the oven fired her blood. She closed the oven door. "French bread."

Neatly sidestepping him, she moved to take the saucepan from the stove. "Dinner won't be ready for a few minutes. If you have something you need to do…"

He hopped up to sit on the island, watching as she poured the tomato mixture into the blender. "Nope. Not a thing."

Resigned to his presence, she switched on the blender, knowing the sound would obliterate any hope he might have of carrying on a conversation with her.

Though the tactic worked, she succeeded only in silencing him, not blinding him. Feeling his gaze, she glanced his way and found him watching her. Self-conscious, she threaded her hair behind her ear. "What?"

His smile was slow and sexy, totally out of character for her boss. "Nothing. I was just noticing how pretty you are."

She snorted a breath. "Right." She poured the contents of the blender into bowls. "I've worked for you for four months and you've never looked at me before?"

"Not in the way I'm seeing you now."

His voice had dropped a level, and for a moment she couldn't think what to say. Taking advantage of her numbed state, he slid down from the counter and looped his arms around her waist.

"I like your mouth. It's—" he dipped his head and brushed his lips over hers "—kissable."

So much for pretending the kiss had never happened, she thought, and resolved herself to her second option, taking ownership for her participation in the kiss. "Listen, Vince—"

"I'll bet you were a cheerleader."

She blinked, thrown off for a moment by the sudden change in topic. "Well, yeah. In high school." She stiffened her spine, determined to say what she had to say. "We need to talk."

He slid his hands down her hips to her thighs. "You're built like a cheerleader. Tight body. Muscular legs."

Her knees turned to water as his fingers trailed down her thighs and back up. Determined to reestablish their employee-boss relationship, she cleared her throat. "About this afternoon…"

Smiling, he brought his hands back to cup her buttocks. "Yeah. That was a nice little surprise."

She swallowed hard, trying her best to ignore the heat that churned in her belly. "I—I think I had too much sun."

His brows drew together. "Did you burn?"

If she'd had a frying pan, she would've bopped him over the head with it. Frustrated, she pushed from his arms. "No, I didn't burn! What I'm trying to tell you is, *yes,* I responded to your kiss, but it was a mistake and it won't happen again."

"Why not?"

She picked up their bowls and headed for the table. "Because it was a mistake."

He trailed after her. "Where's the mistake? I enjoyed it. You obviously enjoyed it."

She slammed a bowl down at one end of the table, then slanted him a scowl, and seated herself at the opposite end and opened her napkin over her lap. "Some things are best forgotten and never repeated."

He snatched up his own napkin and sat, fisting it on his thigh. "Fine. As far as I'm concerned, it never happened."

Smiling, she scooped up a spoonful of soup. "Good, then we agree."

"Something's burning."

She glanced up, then swore and scraped back her chair. "The bread!"

She flung open the oven door and smoke billowed out. Using her napkin as a mitt, she pulled out the tray of blackened bread and ran to dump it in the sink. As an added measure, she threw up the window above the sink to clear the air, then sagged weakly against the counter.

"Did it burn?"

She turned slowly to find Vince still seated at the table and calmly spooning up soup. That he would leave her to deal with the disaster didn't surprise her, but it darn sure made her mad. "Yes," she said tersely.

"That's too bad. It might've made this soup a little more palatable."

Four

After putting on her nightgown, Sally sank down on the edge of her bed to scan the instruction sheet the doctor had provided for any references to concussion:

"Awaken every two hours for first twenty-four hours."

Relieved that she wouldn't have to worry about a repeat performance of the previous night's drama, she set the papers aside and went to the bathroom to collect her cell phone from its hiding place in her makeup bag. Finding four new messages displayed, she brought the cell to her room with her and crawled into bed. Propped against pillows, she punched in the code to retrieve her voice mail, then settled back and brought the phone to her ear.

"Hey, Sally. It's Stacy."

The cheery sound of her coworker's voice made her smile.

"Don't forget tomorrow is Mark's birthday. The party is going to be at lunch and you're in charge of getting the cake."

"Oh, no," Sally moaned, having completely forgotten about the party.

"We're starting early—eleven sharp—which should give us time to hide all the evidence before Captain Friendly gets back in town."

Sally smothered a laugh at the nickname Vince's employees called him behind his back, one she'd picked up on and used herself, since it suited him so well. Making a mental note to call Stacy first thing in the morning and explain the situation to her, she deleted the message, then lifted the phone to her ear again.

"Hey, baby. It's Brad."

She hissed a breath at the sound of her ex's voice.

"Just wanted to let you know I hadn't forgotten about paying back the loan. The job I told you about didn't pan out."

Do they ever? she thought resentfully.

"Turned out the boss was a jerk. But don't worry. I've already got another one lined up. Supposed to go in tomorrow to take the drug test, complete the paperwork, that kind of thing. Puts me in kind of a bind moneywise, though, since I won't be drawing a check for at least two weeks. If you could spare me a couple of hundred bucks, I'll pay you back the first of the month, I swear. I—"

Scowling, she snatched the phone from her ear and punched the delete button.

"Like I'm going to give you any more money," she muttered, and lifted the phone to listen to the next message.

"I hope getting the answering machine isn't an indication you've killed my patient."

She chuckled at the teasing in Dr. O'Connor's voice.

"Just wanted to check in and see how you and Vince were getting along. If you need anything or have any questions, don't hesitate to call me. I wrote my home and cell numbers on the instructions I gave you. Tell Vince that if he's a good boy, I'll give him a sucker the next time I see him."

Shaking her head, she deleted the message then brought the phone back to her ear to listen to the last message.

"Hi, this is Stephanie Parker. This message is for Vince Donnelly. You don't know me, Mr. Donnelly, but our fathers served together in Vietnam."

She lifted a brow. Vietnam? Heavens, talk about a voice from the past! That war ended over thirty years ago.

"My father, Lt. Larry Blair, received a portion of a document prior to leaving for Vietnam and I think your father received one, too. Supposedly, when combined, the pieces of paper are valuable, though their worth can't truly be determined until they're joined.

"It's taken me quite a while to track you down, so I'd appreciate it if you would give me a call at your earliest convenience, as there are others who have an interest in this matter. My number is…"

Sally quickly saved the message and disconnected

the phone. Talk about intrigue, she thought. A missing piece of paper. Unknown value. Others have an interest. Everything about the message was so…well, mysterious! And no one loved a good mystery more than Sally Gregg. She debated going straight to Vince's room and waking him up, so she could find out what he knew about the piece of paper.

"Bad idea," she told herself and leaned to place the cell phone on the nightstand. She wasn't taking a chance on waking him and suffering through another night as his personal teddy bear. Besides, he couldn't return the woman's call tonight. It was too late. It'll keep, she told herself, and switched off the lamp.

But come morning, he was going to tell her every juicy detail about the missing piece of paper, even if she had to resort to torture to make him talk.

She snuggled beneath the covers and closed her eyes. Instead of counting sheep to induce sleep, she imagined all the methods of torture she could use on Vince. Bamboo shoots beneath the nails. Dripping water. Bright lights. Sleep deprivation.

And slept like a baby.

The next morning Sally paced the kitchen, impatient for Vince to wake up. Her mind reeled with questions pertaining to the mysterious phone call. What message did the piece of paper hold? What secret would it reveal when joined with the others the woman had mentioned?

She glanced up at the wall clock and stifled a groan when she saw that it was almost eight o'clock. Was the man going to sleep all day? She'd give him until eight-thirty, she told herself, then she was dragging him out of bed.

In hopes of making the time pass more quickly, she pulled her cell phone from her jeans pocket and dialed the neighborhood supermarket. After placing her order for the groceries she wanted delivered, she then called Stacy to tell her about Vince's trip to the emergency room, him coercing her into taking care of him and the fact that the two of them would be out of the office for the week. Though Stacy commiserated with Sally's predicament, she didn't offer to take her place. Not that Sally blamed her. If Stacy was the one stuck playing nursemaid to Vince, Sally wouldn't have offered, either.

She glanced at the clock again and saw that she'd only managed to burn ten minutes. Twenty more, she told herself and began unloading the dishwasher. It was a mindless task that gave her the opportunity to mull over possible explanations for the piece of paper.

A treasure map? She quickly discarded the idea as too piratelike and too antiquated a concept for the twenty-first century. It had to be some kind of pact, she decided. A secret agreement the soldiers had made before leaving for Vietnam. She toyed with that angle, letting her mind run with the possibilities.

Why would a bunch of soldiers need to make an agreement? Could something have happened while they served together? Maybe a murder they'd covered up? She shivered at the thought, as she pulled soup bowls from the dishwasher. A group of soldiers out drinking and having a good time. Two get into a fight over a woman. One of them whips out a knife. A vicious stab and a soldier dies. The soldier who dealt the killing blow panics and makes his buddies who witnessed the fight sign a pledge of silence.

"What's for breakfast?"

Sally shrieked and bobbled the bowls, barely managing to keep from dropping them. She set them carefully on the counter, then slapped a hand over her heart and whirled to face Vince. "You nearly scared the life out of me."

He headed for the refrigerator. "Who'd you expect? A murderer?"

Because that was exactly what was on her mind, she shuddered at the suggestion, then gaped when she realized that he was wearing a suit, a dead giveaway that he was planning to go to the office, in spite of his doctor's orders.

She would have put an end to that nonsense right then and there, but feared a confrontation would jeopardize her chances of getting him to tell her about the mysterious piece of paper. Choosing to ignore his manner of dress...for the moment, anyway, she said, "You got a call last night."

He lifted his head to frown at her over the open refrigerator door. "I thought you said my cell phone was gone?"

Oops, she thought, then plunged on, deciding it safer to ignore his question. "A woman called. Stephanie Parker, I think she said. Anyway, her father served in Vietnam with yours, and she wants to know if your father has a piece of paper like the one her father has."

Scowling, he yanked out a jug of orange juice and strode to the cabinet.

"Well?" she prodded. "Does he?"

"Don't know and, furthermore, don't care."

Stunned by his response, for a moment she could only stare. She quickly gave herself a shake and hurried to pull a glass from the cabinet, holding it for him while he poured. "But she said it might be valuable."

He snorted. "If my father was involved, I assure you it's worthless."

"How can you know that?"

He took the glass from him her and lifted it in a salute. "Trust me. I know."

"But, Vince—"

"Forget it, Sally. I certainly intend to."

Her jaw sagged. "You mean, you're not going to call her back?"

He took a swig of juice, backhanded the moisture from his mouth. "Nope."

"But you have to! She said there are others involved, and they're all anxious to talk to you."

"I just bet they are," he said dryly and turned for the den.

She charged after him. "I can't believe you're not going to return her call. That's just plain rude."

He spun to face her. "What I do or don't do is no business of yours. None of this is."

Surprised by his anger, she backed up a step. "Okay. Right. It's none of my business." But she couldn't help adding, "But I still think it's rude."

He shot her a scowl, then headed for the mud room

and the garage beyond. She hunched her shoulders and waited for the explosion she knew was coming.

"Sally!"

"Yes, Vince?" she called meekly.

He appeared in the doorway, his face flushed with anger. "Where the hell are the keys to my car?"

"I hid them."

He hauled in a furious breath, then spun back into the mud room. She listened while he yanked open drawers, slammed them shut. When he appeared again, his face was red, his tie askew.

"I mean it, Sally," he warned her. "I want those keys *now*."

Ignoring him, she opened the pantry door. "I hope you like cereal. That's all we have left to eat."

She went through the motions of getting out bowls and filling them with cereal, but was prepared to defend herself, should the need arise. She could hear his heavy breathing, all but feel the daggers of anger he was shooting into her back.

"I called the supermarket," she said, with a calm that belied the nerves jumping in her stomach. "They'll be delivering groceries later this morning. I hope you don't mind," she added, "but I charged them to you. I ordered quite a bit. Since we're going to be here a week, I figured I'd better stock up."

She waited, expecting him to explode at any second, or at the very least, shout curses at her. Instead he strode past her and yanked out a chair at the kitchen table.

"Don't try putting any of that damn yogurt in my cereal," he snapped. "I want *milk*."

She released the breath she'd been holding. "Yes, sir, milk it is."

The morning passed in an unexpected calm. Sally didn't know how Vince spent his time, but she passed hers sitting on the sofa, thumbing through her stash of magazines while waiting on the groceries to be delivered. She flagged pages of a couple of recipes that piqued her interest and read with amusement an article promising "Fifteen minutes a day and no more poochy stomach!"

Hearing a vehicle on the drive, she set aside the magazine and hurried to the front door. Before opening it, she looked out the peephole to verify it was the delivery truck. She choked a breath when she saw Vince dart from the shrubbery alongside the drive and approach the delivery van.

She yanked open the door and stormed out to intercept him, knowing full well he wasn't there to offer his help in unloading the groceries. Since he had a head start, he reached the van before she did and was passing the driver an envelope when she arrived.

She plucked the envelope from the driver's hand. "Shame on you, Vince," she scolded. "Trying to bribe this nice man into buying you drugs, when you know the last person you tried to get to do your dirty work for you is currently serving time in prison."

The driver threw up his hands. "Whoa. Wait a minute.

I don't know anything about no drugs. Swear to God. All he said was for me to take the envelope and open it later. I thought he was giving me a tip for delivering the groceries."

She gave the driver's arm a reassuring pat. "Don't worry. I don't blame you." She narrowed an eye at Vince. "*He's* the one with the problem."

The driver dragged an arm over the perspiration that beaded his forehead. "I'll just get these groceries unloaded and get out of your hair."

"Thank you—" she glanced at the name embroidered on the front of his shirt, then back up at him and smiled "—Bill. Just leave the boxes on the porch."

Taking Vince by the arm, she hustled him toward the house, saying for the driver's benefit, "You should be ashamed of yourself. Trying to bribe that nice man. Honestly. I can't take my eyes off you for a minute without you getting into trouble."

The envelope contained two crisp one-hundred-dollar bills and a scrawled note, requesting the driver return at midnight and pick up Vince. God only knew what Vince had planned to do once he escaped, Sally thought, as she tore up the note and dumped it in the wastebasket. Vowing to keep a more diligent watch on her patient in the future, she marched down the hall to his bedroom and rapped once on the door.

"Go away," came his muffled reply.

Pursing her lips, she thrust open the door. Vince stood before the window, an arm braced along the frame, staring out. "Try that again," she informed him, "and I'm calling Dr. O'Connor."

He shot her a scowl over his shoulder, then turned his face to the window again. "Call him, the hospital would be better than staying in this hell hole with you."

"Then why don't you go back and save us both a lot of grief?"

He dropped his arm and crossed to the bed, stripping off his suit coat. "Save *you* some grief, you mean," he grumbled.

"Oh, for heaven's sake, Vince. Do you honestly believe I'm enjoying all this? Acting as your nursemaid and warden isn't how I'd choose to spend my week, I promise you. Listening to you moan and groan about how bored you are, how rotten the food is. Being manhandled every time I turn around."

A small smile chipped at the corner of his mouth. "Manhandled?"

"Yes, manhandled!" she said furiously. "And if you think I'm going to put up with any more of your shenanigans, you're crazy." Realizing she was yelling, she stopped and hauled in a deep breath. "Now," she said, feeling somewhat calmer. "I'm going to put away the groceries. If you're truly as bored as you claim, you might consider helping."

Leaving him to stew, she headed for the porch where the deliveryman had left the boxes of groceries. She lifted the first, straining a bit beneath its weight, and carried it to the kitchen. She hefted the box up onto the island counter and turned to fetch another.

And bumped smack up against Vince.

She quickly stepped aside, allowing him room to place the box he held on the counter.

"You put the groceries away, I'll carry."

She lifted a brow, surprised by his offer. "Okay. Sure."

While he went to collect another box, she began sorting the groceries into two categories: refrigerated and pantry. She was wiping off the refrigerator shelves, before replenishing the stock, when he returned with the last box.

"If you weren't here, what would you be doing?"

She lifted her head to peer at him over the door, surprised by the question. "I'd be at work."

He picked up a can and juggled it in his hand, avoiding her gaze. "I mean after hours."

Doing laundry, grocery shopping, watching television. But she wasn't about to tell him that. It made her life sound so incredibly boring.

With a shrug, she tossed the dishcloth into the sink and scooped up the gallon of skim milk. "I don't know. I don't have any set schedule."

"Do you have a boyfriend?"

Uncomfortable, she angled the milk onto a shelf in the refrigerator. "No one special," she said vaguely, then flipped the question back at him. "Do you have a girlfriend?"

He shook his head. "Too restrictive."

She sputtered a laugh. "What's that supposed to mean?"

Frowning, he dragged up a bar stool and sat down, but kept his gaze on the label of the can he still held.

"Women make demands, expect things I don't have the time or inclination to give."

She lifted a brow. "Is that experience speaking or simply a generalization you've drawn from watching your friends?"

"I only have one friend. Pat."

"Your own experience, then."

"I suppose, although I've never been involved in what you'd call a serious relationship. Not that I lack for female companionship," he was to quick to tell her. "I just prefer to keep things loose. You know, friendly. No strings or rings."

He smiled, as if it was a fond memory. "There was one exception. Becky Thornton. We were fourth grade sweethearts. I gave her a plastic ring I got out of one of those quarter toy machines. Two weeks later she dumped me for Pete Peters. Broke my heart."

"Young hearts are fragile," she stated prosaically.

Heaving a sigh, he rose and carried the can to pantry. "Yeah, I suppose."

Though he said nothing more, Sally kept a surreptitious eye on him as he helped her put away the remaining groceries. She didn't know what to think of his somber mood or the unexpected glimpse into his life he'd provided. Could it be a ruse? she wondered. A diversion to keep her from watching him too closely? A ploy to earn her sympathy?

Deciding it safest not to lower her guard, she picked up the empty boxes. "I'm going to put these in the garage. Do you want to play cards or something when I get back?"

He lifted a shoulder. "I suppose."

Frustrated by his lack of enthusiasm, she carried the boxes to the garage. When she returned, she found him in the den, sifting through the contents of the black lacquered bookcase that lined the far wall. "What are you looking for?" she asked curiously.

"This," he said and pulled out a box.

She looked from the game to him. "Monopoly?"

"Used to play it all the time when I was a kid."

He sat down on the sofa and placed the box on the coffee table in front of him. "I'll be the banker," he said, as he opened the board. "Which game piece do you want?"

She sat down beside him, watching as he placed stacks of cards on labeled squares on the center of the board. "What are my choices?"

He angled his head to peer at her. "Are you serious?"

Pursing her lips, she snatched up the token closest to her, which happened to be a replica of a vintage iron. "This will do."

He hid a smile. "Figures."

"What's wrong with the iron?" she asked indignantly.

Lifting a shoulder, he selected the money bag token for himself and placed it on Start. "Nothing that I'm aware of." He hid a smile. "But I'd imagine a psychologist could fill a book with all it says about your personality."

"No!" Sally cried and slapped at Vince's hand. "You can't take Park Place! That's the best property I own."

After hours of playing, they'd moved the board to the floor and now lay on their stomachs opposite each other.

Vince plucked the deed from her side of the board. "Rule's a rule. If you land on my property and can't pay the rent, you have to mortgage what you own."

"Greedy gut," she grumbled.

"Sticks and stones…"

Rolling to her back, she flung out her arms in defeat. "I give up. You win."

"You can't quit now."

She tipped her head back and shot him an upside-down frown. "Watch me."

"Come on, Sal. The game's just getting interesting."

"For you, maybe. It lost its allure for me about three hours ago."

"Here," he said, and tossed the deed to Park Place back to her side of the board. "I'll let you keep your real estate."

"Why? So I can lose it to you on my next roll?"

"I'll make you a loan. Interest free," he added.

"Why can't you just let me admit defeat and be done with it?"

"Where's the fun in that?"

"When the alternative is being bled dry and having a victory dance performed on my dead carcass? I consider it a blast."

He hopped to his feet and rounded the board. "Tell you what," he said, and extended a hand. "We'll take a break. Do something else for a while, then pick up the game where we left off."

Eyeing him warily, she allowed him to pull her up. "Like what?"

"You choose. Whatever you want."

"And you'll participate?"

"As long as you agree to finish the game we started."

She stuck out her hand. "You've got yourself a deal."

After sealing the agreement with a shake, he stuffed his hands in his pockets and rocked back on his heels. "So what's it going to be? Cards? Dominoes? I may have a chess set somewhere."

"I was thinking kick ball."

He blinked. "Kick ball?"

"Yeah. Didn't you ever play that as a kid?"

"Well, yeah. I'm sure I must have at one time or another."

"I've got a soccer ball in my trunk. I'll get it."

When she started around him, he held up a hand. "Wait. You carry a soccer ball around in the trunk of your car?"

"I play in a league on the weekends. Keeps me in shape." She clapped him on the back, as she passed by him. "You might want to change. Kick ball's hard on clothes."

Vince wondered if she'd chosen the game to kill him, because he was fairly certain he was going to die. His T-shirt was soaked with sweat, his calves screaming.

And they'd only been at it for ten minutes.

He wasn't out of shape, he told himself. It was just that she was so *in* shape.

"Ready?" she called.

He lined up on the lawn twenty feet opposite her, ball in hand. "As ready as I'll ever be." Poised like a bowler eyeing the headpin for a strike, he brought his arm back, then swung it forward and sent the ball rolling toward her. She pulled her leg back as if she intended to kick the ball to the moon…but punted softly instead.

Cursing himself for falling for such an obvious ruse, he raced forward, trying to catch the ball while it was still in the air. It hit the ground two feet in front of him. Swearing, he scooped it up.

"Bet you can't catch me," Sally taunted, then took off at a run.

With a clear shot at her, Vince pulled his arm back, but just as he started to release the ball, she darted to the left and into the cover of trees. He quickly tucked the ball under his arm and took off after her, ruing the day he'd bought a house with two acres of landscaped grounds.

She led him on a chase that took him to areas of his property he'd never seen, before changing her route and heading toward the house. When she reached the pool deck, she turned to taunt him again. Vince didn't even hesitate. Letting out a lionlike roar, he dropped the ball and charged. He saw her eyes widen in alarm, but she wasn't able to react in time. Grabbing her up, while still at a full run, he carried her with him into the pool.

They plunged beneath the surface, sending water shooting up like a geyser. The weight of their joined bodies, combined with the speed at which they'd hit the water, sent them on a torpedolike journey to the bottom. She kicked and pushed at him, trying to break free, but he merely hooked his leg around hers and tightened his hold, making any kind of movement impossible.

Slowly he became aware of the intimacy of their

position. Chests, groin, arms, legs—they were as tightly entwined as any two lovers.

With his gaze locked on hers, he knew the instant she became aware of that fact, too. He saw her eyes sharpen, felt the kick of her heartbeat against his chest, the swell of her breasts against his chest. His toe scraped the bottom of the pool and he pushed off, knowing he was going to have to kiss her. How could he resist when her mouth was right in front of him and her body molded his like a glove?

Five

Sally felt as if she were submerged in a dream, the only sound the hollow echo of water lapping overhead, the only illumination shimmering crystals of light that danced on the walls of the pool.

But the man opposite her was part of no dream.

She felt the pressure of his hand at her neck and closed her eyes as he brought her face to his, knowing he was going to kiss her. The first touch of his mouth sent a jolt through her system that had her arching instinctively against him. Though her lungs burned for much-needed air, her muscles for release from the human constraints that bound her, she melted against him and returned his kiss.

As they broke through the surface, she tore her mouth

from his, gasping, to meet his gaze. Water streamed in narrow rivulets down his face, fell like rain from his chin. Mesmerized by the glittering beads of moisture that clung to his lips, she leaned to capture them with her tongue. With a groan, he crushed his mouth over hers again. Heat flamed in her middle and spread through her bloodstream, quickening nerves dormant for far too many years.

Slowly she became aware of the water creeping higher and higher on her neck and struggled to free her legs, desperate to remain afloat so the kiss wouldn't end. He must have sensed them sinking, too, because he locked an arm around her waist and used the other like an oar to pull them toward the shallower end of the pool. Once able to stand, he brought her up with him and locked her legs around his hips. Gripping his hands at her ribs, he lifted her high and opened his mouth over a breast. She dropped her head back on a soft cry of pleasure as he suckled, each new sensation more exquisite, more electrifying than the one before.

Though her body cried out for more, all but demanded it, she knew she had to stop this madness before she completely lost control.

"Vince. Please," she begged. "We can't do this."

When he ignored her, she caught his head between her hands and forced his face up to hers. "No," she said firmly.

He stared at her a long moment, as if weighing his chances of changing her mind, then reluctantly lowered her to her feet. "Okay, but you don't know what you're missing."

His response was totally egotistical and exactly what she might've expected from him, but she had a feeling it was based on fact, not brag.

"Unfortunately, I think I do."

After showering and changing into dry clothes, Sally went straight to the den, intending to put the Monopoly board away, before Vince could demand they resume their game. Unfortunately, he beat her there and was already stretched out on the floor, waiting for her.

"You don't really want to finish the game, do you?" she asked hopefully.

"Not if we can continue the one we started in the pool."

Pursing her lips, she dropped down on the floor opposite him.

He picked up the dice. "As I recall, it was my turn." He gave the dice a shake, then opened his hand and sent them tumbling across the board. He moved his game piece the allotted seven spaces the dice had earned him, which landed him on Community Chest. He drew a card from the stack, read it and burst out laughing.

Sally eyed him warily. "What's so funny?"

Instead of telling her, he handed her the card to read for herself.

"Bank error in your favor. Collect $200."

She passed the card back to him. "What's so funny about that?"

He gave her slim holdings a pointed look as he slipped the card beneath the bottom of the stack. "You know how the saying goes. 'The rich get richer and the poor get poorer.'"

Irritated by his cavalier attitude, she snatched up the dice. "You could show a little compassion, you know."

"Compassion is for the weak and foolish."

She glanced up. "You don't really mean that."

"Damn right I do." He took two one-hundred-dollar bills from the bank and added it to his stash. "You don't get anywhere in this world filling every empty hand that's thrust your way."

"So you just turn your back on hunger and need? Pretend it's not there?"

"Why should I feel an obligation to feed and clothe the world? I didn't create the need."

She slowly pushed up to an elbow, unable to believe he would say something so heartless, so unbelievably selfish. "People don't *choose* poverty. Sometimes they're dragged into it by circumstances completely out of their control."

"Like I said, I didn't create the need."

"Maybe not, but those with means have a responsibility to help the less fortunate."

He picked up the dice and set them on the board in front of her with a *click*, then looked up to meet her gaze. "Says who?"

She stared, chilled to the bone by the coldness in his eyes, then scowled and snatched up the dice. "Your parents screwed up big-time raising you."

"My beliefs are my own."

"That may be, but they didn't just pop into your head

fully developed. They were formed over the years. More than likely by your parents. Judging by your attitude, my guess is they spoiled you rotten."

He clamped his hand over hers, his fingers cutting deep. "I was never spoiled. If anything, I was robbed of what should've been mine."

Stunned by his anger, she said slowly, "Okay. Sure. Whatever you say."

He released her and the dice fell from her numb fingers.

"Three," he said tersely and moved her game piece for her. "That puts you on Baltic, which I own. With two hotels, that means you owe me $900." He lifted his gaze to hers. "How much have you got?"

She looked down at her remaining cash and the two properties she held. "Forty in cash, plus mortgage values...roughly 280."

He picked up the board and dumped the game pieces into the box. "I win."

Sally couldn't sleep that night. Her mind kept replaying her conversation with Vince and searching for an explanation for his lack of compassion, his ruthlessness. It was an impossible task, as she knew very little about him and nothing at all about his family. Yet she firmly believed his parents were responsible for forming his beliefs, no matter how vehemently he denied it. No one was born that cold-blooded and uncaring.

Frustrated, she sat up and switched on the lamp beside her bed. Raking her fingers through her hair, she held her head, while trying to remember anything Vince had said, even in passing, that might offer a clue as to why he was the way he was.

Prior to the current week, her conversations with her boss were limited to those conducted at the office and usually related to his business in some way or another. He rarely, if ever, discussed his personal life and never mentioned his family.

She wouldn't have known about his mother, if her secretarial duties hadn't included paying his bills, one of which was from the Alzheimer center where his mother was confined. She knew his father was deceased, but she'd only made that discovery—

She tensed, remembering the conversation she'd had with Vince about his father. When she'd told him about the phone call and asked him about the missing piece of paper, he'd said he didn't know and didn't care. And when she'd insisted that it might be valuable, he had said…what? she asked herself in frustration. Something like, if his father was involved, the paper was worthless.

He'd seemed certain of its lack of value and adamant in his refusal to discuss his father, which led her to believe a breach of some kind had occurred between the two. Was that why Vince was the way he was? she wondered. Did it all lead back to his father?

She slumped her shoulders, knowing she stood little chance of ever finding out, since Vince refused to discuss his father.

Firming her jaw, she swung her legs over the side of the bed. "There's more than one way to skin a cat," she muttered as she lifted the mattress and dug out the laptop she'd concealed beneath it. Computer in hand, she crawled back into bed, flipped open the lid and connected to the Internet. She knew it was a long shot, but she searched "Vince Donnelly Texas son of" and was pleasantly surprised when her search earned her six hits. The first took her to the Web site of the *Houston Post* and an article regarding Vince's procurement of an export company located in Hong Kong. Finding the information she needed in the next to last paragraph, she quickly copied Vincent Donnelly, Vince's father's name, and pasted it into the box and clicked Search. Her eyes shot wide when 11,636 results appeared.

Realizing the impossibility of checking them all, she added "Texas" to the parameters, in hopes of narrowing the list, and was disappointed when it reduced the field by a measly 3,000. Resigning herself to the task, she clicked the first link. When the new screen opened, she gaped, thinking for a moment she was looking at a picture of her boss surrounded by a group of children. A quick check of the caption beneath the photo identified the man in the picture as Vincent Donnelly, Vince's father. The resemblance between the two was uncanny, and served as visible proof that Vince had inherited his features and coloring from his father, as well as his name.

More intrigued than ever, Sally studied the photo, trying to find Vince among the children gathered around his father. But not one of the children resembled Vince. With a shrug, she read the accompanying article.

Hours later she closed her laptop and pressed her fingers against eyes that burned from staring at a computer screen too long, and tried to assimilate all that she'd learned about Vince's dad. That he was famous was without question—not movie-star famous—but definitely well known in the State of Texas. "Vietnam veteran singlehandedly takes on the rehabilitation and care of thousands of other less fortunate vets." That was only one of hundreds of accolades attributed to Vince's dad.

She dropped her hands to her lap in frustration. How could anyone *not* like a man like Vincent Donnelly? A man who'd worked tirelessly for the benefit of disabled veterans, as well as the widows and orphans of soldiers who didn't make it home from the Vietnam War? She'd think Vince would be *proud* of the work his father had done. Without the backing of any charitable organization or corporation, his father had dedicated himself to changing the lives of hundreds, maybe thousands in a positive way. Yet, if anything, Vince seemed bitter toward his father, even resentful.

Resentful? Her eyes sharpened, as her mind zeroed in on the emotion and called up Vince's reaction when she'd accused him of being spoiled by his parents. She'd never forget the fury in his eyes, the defiant set of his jaw.

I was never spoiled. If anything, I was robbed of what should've been mine.

At the time, she'd thought by *robbed* he'd meant an inheritance of some kind. But now she wondered if he'd been referring to something less tangible. Specifically his father's attention and love. She could see how it might have happened. Good grief! She'd just spent hours reading articles and records pertaining to the work

GET FREE BOOKS and FREE GIFTS WHEN YOU PLAY THE...

Lucky 7

777

Just scratch off the silver box with a coin. Then check below to see the gifts you get!

SLOT MACHINE GAME!

YES!
I have scratched off the silver box. Please send me the 2 free Silhouette Desire® books and 2 free gifts for which I qualify. I understand I am under no obligation to purchase any books, as explained on the back of this card.

326 SDL ELYM　　　　　　　　　　**225 SDL ELQA**

FIRST NAME	LAST NAME

ADDRESS

APT.#	CITY

STATE/PROV.	ZIP/POSTAL CODE

7	7	7	**Worth TWO FREE BOOKS** plus 2 BONUS Mystery Gifts!
🍒	🍒	🍒	**Worth TWO FREE BOOKS!**
♣	♣	♣	**Worth ONE FREE BOOK!**
🔔	🔔	🍒	**TRY AGAIN!**

www.eHarlequin.com

(S-D-05/07)

DETACH AND MAIL CARD TODAY!

© 2000 HARLEQUIN ENTERPRISES LTD ® and TM are trademarks owned and used by the trademark owner and/or its licensee.

The Silhouette Reader Service™ — Here's how it works:

Accepting your 2 free books and 2 free mystery gifts places you under no obligation to buy anything. You may keep the books and gifts and return the shipping statement marked "cancel". If you do not cancel, about a month later we'll send you 6 additional books and bill you just $3.80 each in the U.S. or $4.47 each in Canada, plus 25¢ shipping & handling per book and applicable taxes if any.* That's the complete price and — compared to cover prices of $4.50 each in the U.S. and $5.25 each in Canada — it's quite a bargain! You may cancel at any time, but if you choose to continue, every month we'll send you 6 more books, which you may either purchase at the discount price or return to us and cancel your subscription.

*Terms and prices subject to change without notice. Sales tax applicable in N.Y. Canadian residents will be charged applicable provincial taxes and GST. All orders subject to approval. Credit or debit balances in a customer's account(s) may be offset by any other outstanding balance owed by or to the customer. Please allow 4 to 6 weeks for delivery.

Vincent Donnelly had done for the benefit of others, and she was sure what information she'd found online was nowhere near a complete accounting of his accomplishments. That kind of dedication took commitment and time. Time he might very well have stolen from his family.

She frowned thoughtfully, trying to remember if any of the articles she'd read had mentioned Vince or his mother, but couldn't recall a single one.

Was that why Vince was so resentful? she wondered. Was it because he felt his father had spent more time with strangers than he had his own son?

Saddened by the possibility, she switched off her lamp and pulled her covers to her chin.

She remembered when her mother had died, going through a period of anger in which she had blamed her mother for leaving her. It was her grandmother who had eventually made her understand that her mother hadn't *chosen* to leave Sally. Death had made the choice for her.

Was it possible that Vince's anger toward his father was in some way similar to what Sally had felt toward her mother? Did he resent the time his father had spent away from home? Did he feel as if his father had cared more for the people he helped than he did for his own child?

She remembered the first photo she'd found on the Internet, the one with Vince's father surrounded by children. Vince hadn't been among those gathered around him. She could imagine him standing just outside of camera range, watching and wishing his father would give him the same attention.

Careful, she warned herself, when she felt her heart

softening toward Vince. She was already physically attracted to her boss. That was dangerous enough. But she could deal with the attraction. Once she was back in her own apartment and working at the office, rather than at Vince's home, whatever attraction she felt toward him would die a natural death.

But if she allowed herself to care for him, let her heart soften toward him…well, that was just asking for trouble.

A loud crash jerked Sally from sleep.

Wide-eyed, she eased from the bed and tiptoed to the door to press her ear against the wood. Though muted, she could hear the distinct sound of footsteps in another part of the house, the sound of objects being picked up and discarded.

Sure that a burglar was in the house, she carefully twisted open the knob and peered out. Seeing no one in sight, she glanced across the hall at Vince's closed door. She considered waking him and letting him deal with the burglar, but decided against it. He'd taken one of the sedatives before going to bed and she knew from experience he'd be of little help to her now.

She took a cautious step out into the hallway, a second, then stopped to listen again. She heard another crash, a muffled "Dammit!"

Recognizing the voice as Vince's, she set her jaw and marched to the front of the house, where she found him in his office, shining a flashlight inside file drawers whose contents were scattered on the floor around his feet.

Bracing a shoulder against the doorjamb, she flipped on the overhead light. "Lose something?"

He bobbled the flashlight, then scowled and switched it off. "I want my laptop."

"Sorry. Can't have it."

"Come on, Sally," he whined. "I've got business to take care of. The Holt deal for one. They're expecting an analysis by Friday."

"Mark's taking care of that."

He snorted a breath. "Mark can't add two and two and get four."

She raised a brow. "Really? I'm sure his professors at Harvard would be surprised to hear that, considering he graduated with honors from their business school."

"It takes more than a degree to know how to pull a company out of bankruptcy and into the black."

"I'm sure it does, and I would assume Mark has those qualities or you never would have hired him."

When he only scowled, she tossed up her hands. "I don't understand why you have all these people working for you if you won't let them do the jobs you've hired them to do."

"Control is crucial to success."

"Micromanaging your employees is a waste of your talent and time," she retorted.

He slowly turned his head to look at her. "Is that what you think I do? Micromanage?"

She lifted her chin, knowing full well she was overstepping her bounds as his secretary, and possibly putting her job on the line. "Yes, I do. All your employees, including Mark, are intelligent and experts in their field, and if you don't start trusting them to do their jobs, showing them a little respect, you're going to lose them to someone who will."

"Do I micromanage you, as well?"

She wet her lips, uncomfortable now that he had shifted the attention to her. "My position is different. It's necessary for us to work closely together. We have to, in order for me to stay abreast of your schedule, meet your needs."

He lifted a brow. "Meet my needs?"

Heat flamed in her cheeks. "You know very well what I mean."

"Do I?" He started toward her.

"Vince…" she warned.

But he kept coming and didn't stop until he was standing in front of her. With his gaze on hers, he reached to thread a lock of hair behind her ear.

"Want to know why I was looking for my laptop?" His voice had dropped at least an octave and sent a shiver chasing down her spine. "Because I couldn't sleep." He drew his hand from her ear to cup her cheek. "Want to know why I couldn't sleep? Because I have a need. A really *big* need."

She swallowed hard. "That's not my problem."

"Oh, I think it is, since you're the one who created it."

She braced her hands against his chest, intending to push him away. "Vince—"

He dipped his head to nuzzle her neck. "Yes, Sally?"

She closed her eyes against the pleasure his mouth stirred, the sensual little nips of his teeth. "Please. Don't."

He looped his arms around her waist. "Don't what, Sally?" he whispered against her lips.

She couldn't think, could barely breathe. Her heart was beating so loudly, she was sure he could hear it. Probably feel it. She could certainly feel his. His chest was bare beneath her palms, his skin warm. The heat it emitted snaked up her arms, wedged in her throat.

She wanted him. She could admit that—never to him, of course. Only to herself. And what woman wouldn't want him? Especially one who had been without a man as long as Sally had. But there was a lot at stake here. Most of all her job.

"I'm a good secretary," she heard herself say.

He flicked his tongue over her lips. "The best. Don't know what I'd do without you."

Unaware that he felt that way, she pushed back to look at him. "You mean that?"

"Of course I do."

"And you wouldn't let…well, *this,* affect my job?"

His smile soft, he caught her hand and drew it to his lips. "I've always managed to keep my business and personal lives separate in the past. I can't see how sleeping with you would change that."

She hesitated a moment longer, unsure whether she should be relieved or insulted by his reply. Choosing relief, she melted against him. "Kiss me again."

He reached to switch off the light. "I have a better idea." Catching the hem of her nightgown, he pulled it up and over her head. The glow from the streetlights filtered through the window and spilled over her breasts. He stared, the gown slipping from his fingers, forgotten. Humming low in his throat, he gathered her breasts between his hands, pressed his face in the valley between.

"You smell like coconuts," he murmured.

She swallowed, trying to find her voice. "Body lotion," she finally managed to say. "Tropical Illusion."

He swept his tongue up to the hollow at the base of her throat, then back down. "I like it."

Weak, she had to brace her hands on his shoulders to remain upright. "Yeah," she said vaguely. "Me, too."

Without warning, he stooped and scooped her up into his arms.

She clamped her arms around his neck. "What are you doing?"

"Taking you to my room. It's bigger, more comfortable and, as an added bonus, we can sleep there afterward."

She couldn't argue with the change in venue, but it seemed ridiculous for him to carry her, when she could just as easily walk. But she let him, deciding she rather liked the gesture. Sort of cavemanish but nice.

Once inside his room, he laid her down on the bed. Her nerves fluttered a bit, as she watched him strip off his silk boxers, but settled as he stretched out over her and pressed his mouth to hers.

Drawing back, he touched a finger to her lips. "Nervous?"

"A little."

"Me, too."

She looked at him doubtfully. "Really?"

Hiding a smile, he brushed his lips over hers. "No. But I thought it would make you feel better if you thought I was."

She had to smile because, true or not, his ploy had worked. She did feel more relaxed.

Her smile faded to an expression of wonder as he stroked a hand over her hair, trailed his fingers over her cheek, her throat. Mesmerized by the gentleness of his touch, the warmth that softened his eyes, she gave herself a moment to enjoy the experience before allowing herself to touch him, as well.

Tentative at first, she splayed her hands over his shoulders but grew bolder and smoothed her palms down his back, over his ribs, dipped her fingertips into the shallow that bordered his hips. Perfection, she thought, with a shuddery sigh, as she brought her hands up to frame a face so incredibly handsome it might have been carved by a sculptor's hand.

His gaze on hers, he slipped a hand between their chests. "So soft," he whispered, as he encircled her breasts.

She arched up, gasping when his thumb grazed her nipple. Humming his approval, he pushed himself down her body, until his face was even with her breasts. Taking them between his hands, he tasted first one then the other, before settling his mouth over the first and drawing it in.

Heat exploded in her middle and she clamped her legs together, fearing she would come apart then and there. As if sensing her growing need, he slipped a hand between her legs and pushed a finger along her fold. Her sex softened at his touch, turned molten.

Flooded by sensation, she pressed her head back, gasping, as he shaped his hand over her mound and squeezed. "Vince," she all but sobbed. "Please. Now."

Stretching over her, he plucked a condom from the drawer of the bedside table and caught a corner of the wrapper between his teeth. His gaze on hers, he tore off a section, then sank back on his heels and offered her the package. "You do the honors."

She pushed herself to an elbow to position the condom over the head of his manhood and gently rolled it down its length. She heard a low moan, and looked up to find his eyes were squeezed shut, his jaw clenched. Realizing his need was as great as hers, she rose higher to wrap her arms around his neck and nipped at his lips.

"Make love with me," she whispered, even as she drew him down over her again.

It was all the invitation he needed.

Slipping a hand beneath her buttocks, he lifted, bringing her hips up to meet his, and pushed inside. Her mouth opened on a silent cry of pleasure as he filled her, closed to smother a moan as he began to move, each thrust taking him deeper and deeper. Shrouded by shadows, blinded by need, she clung to him, riding the crest of a wave that swept her higher.

Heat pulsed around her, inside her, slicked her skin. Desperate for the release only he could give her, she dragged her hands down his back, up along his arms, framed his face, whispering his name over and over again, as she pressed her lips to his mouth, his eyes, his cheeks. She felt the tension that tightened his body, the tremble that shook him from head to toe, and arched high wanting to take that breathtaking plunge with him.

Pleasure ripped through her center, shattered her mind, colored her world. Eyes closed, she inhaled deeply as she floated, savoring his scent, gathering memories to examine later. She felt his hand cup her face, and laced her fingers through his.

"You okay?"

Before she could answer, he drew her hand to his mouth and pressed a kiss against its center. The tenderness in the gesture, the utter sweetness of it, drew tears to her eyes.

She released a shuddery sigh and whispered, "Better than okay."

Six

Vince slept, but there was no way Sally could sleep. Watching him was much more enjoyable.

He looked so cute curled up next to her, it was all she could do to keep her hands to herself. Wisps of hair feathered his forehead, all but begging her to comb them back, and his lower lip pouted as if anticipating her kiss. Unable to resist, she brushed the tip of her finger over the lip's fullness and had to duck when he batted a hand as if swatting at a pesky fly.

Holding her breath, she waited until he'd settled again, then laid her head on the pillow beside his and resigned herself to simply watch. She still found it hard to believe that they'd made love. What amazed her more was discovering what a tender and unselfish lover he'd proven to be. It was such a contradiction to his normal demeanor and made her wonder if there was a gentler, kinder side trapped inside that only needed nurturing to reveal itself.

"Can't sleep?"

Wincing, she laid a hand on his chest. "Sorry. I didn't mean to wake you."

He caught her hand and pulled it to his lips. "You didn't." He guided her hand around his neck, then tugged her close to cuddle. "Why can't you sleep?"

She snuggled against his chest. "I don't know. Just not tired, I guess."

He stroked a hand down her hair. "Regrets?"

She tipped her face up to look at him, then tucked it against his chest again, hiding a smile. "None. You?"

"Only one."

She tensed, then asked uneasily, "What?"

"It was over too damn fast."

She looked up again, to see if he was teasing and saw the glint of humor in his eyes. Laughing, she pushed him to his back and crawled on top of him, pinning his arms to the bed. "Then I guess I'll have to make sure this one lasts a long, long time."

Sally floated lazily, buoyed by the inflated raft beneath her. Vince drifted beside her on a matching raft, his eyes hidden by dark sunglasses. Overhead the sun ducked in and out of puffy white clouds, offering an occasional respite from its blinding heat.

Sally scooped up a handful of water and dribbled it over her middle. "We're nothing but a couple of slugs."

"Speak for yourself. My mind is always working."

She glanced over. "Well, shut it off. You're supposed to be relaxing."

He pushed out his arms and stretched, then dropped them with a sigh to lace his hands over his stomach again. "Can't."

"Sure you can. Think black and it'll go blank."

He looked over the top of his sunglasses at her. "You're kidding, right?"

She sat up, letting her legs dangle over the side of the raft. "Works for me. Picture yourself with a paintbrush painting your mind black." She pushed out a hand. "Go ahead. Try it. You'll see."

His expression doubtful, he dropped his sunglasses back into place and wrinkled his forehead in concentration.

"Black," she reminded him. "Big, bold strokes of black."

She waited a minute. "Well? Is it working?"

"I don't know. It's so dark in here I can't see a thing."

Laughing, she kicked out a foot, splashing water at him. "You're such a—" She squealed as he grabbed her foot and hauled her raft to his.

He held out his hand. "Come here."

She eyed his raft doubtfully. "There's not room enough for two."

He scooted to the opposite side, creating space for her. "Sure there is."

Though she was sure she'd end up in the pool, she held her breath and shifted to his raft, not releasing it until she'd settled safely at his side.

"Satisfied?"

He lifted her head to slip his arm beneath it. "Couldn't be happier."

She slapped at the hand he tried to slip inside her bikini top. "I should've known you had an ulterior motive in wanting me here."

He nuzzled her cheek with his nose. "Can I help it if I find you irresistible?"

Seduced by his voice, she closed her eyes. "Flattery will get you—" Her eyes shot wide, when she sensed cold air hitting her breasts. "Vince!" she cried, slapping her hands against her chest. But it was too late to save her top. Vince was already twirling it over his head. "Vince Donnelly," she said furiously. "You give me that back."

He gave the top another swing, then released it and sent it sailing across the pool. "Let's go skinny-dipping."

Her jaw dropped. "Are you crazy? It's broad daylight!"

"So?" He rolled off the raft and held on to its side. "No one can see us."

Not at all sure she believed him, she slid off the opposite side. "This is insane. *You're* insane."

He stripped off his trunks and tossed them behind him. "Come on, Sal. Admit it. It feels good, doesn't it?"

She wanted to tell him she hated it, was totally miserable and demand that he return her bikini top. Instead, she slid her fingers beneath the elastic of her bottoms and peeled them down her legs. "If you dare tell anyone we did this, I'll cut you up in tiny pieces and feed you to the buzzards."

With a mischievous glint in his eyes, he dived beneath the water. Unsure of his intent, she backed away, watching as he swam nearer and nearer.

"Vince—"

Before she could complete the warning, he grabbed her ankle and dragged her down. Hooking an arm at her waist, he held her against his side, and swam to the deeper end of the pool.

He was right, she thought, and added her stroke to his to speed their journey. Swimming naked *did* feel good. Gliding through the water like a mermaid, with every inch of her body exposed to the pulsating water. It was truly a freeing and totally sensual experience. And Vince… She sent a glance his way. He looked like some kind of nautical god, with his hair streaming behind him and sunlight glinting off his bare skin.

Drawing her to a stand at the bottom of the pool, he pulled her into his arms and closed his mouth over hers. She was sure she could have remained with him there forever.

But a desperate need for air sent them racing to the top. They broke through the surface together, both laughing like fools.

"Having a good time?"

The voice came from behind Sally, and since she was looking straight at Vince, she knew he wasn't the one who had spoken. She slowly turned to find Dr. O'Connor standing at the edge of the pool. The blood drained from her face, then shot right back up to paint her cheeks a vivid red.

Obviously not sharing her embarrassment, Vince slung an arm over her shoulders. "Hey, Pat. Come on in and join us."

She snapped her gaze to Vince, her eyes filled with horror. He just smiled and gave her bare butt a reassuring pat.

Hiding a smile, Dr. O'Connor shook his head. "Sorry. I'll have to take a rain check. I'm on my way to the hospital. Just dropped by to see how the two of you were getting along." He lifted a brow. "But looks like you're doing just fine." Hiding a smile, he touched a finger to his forehead and turned away. "Mind the sun," he called over his shoulder. "I'd hate for y'all to burn."

The minute she heard the gate close behind him, Sally dropped her face to her hands. "Oh, God," she moaned pitifully. "I could just die."

"Why? It's not like Pat's never seen a naked woman before. He's a doctor."

She dropped her hands to glare. "He's never seen *me*."

He rolled his lips inward, trying not to laugh. "He has now."

Sally felt the bed vibrating and knew Vince was laughing again. She poked him hard in the ribs. "Would you stop? It's not funny."

He patted the air between them. "Sorry. Really. It's

just that every time I think about the look on your face when you heard Pat's voice…"

She flopped to her side, turning her back to him. "I never should have let you talk me into going skinny-dipping in the first place."

"Didn't take much talking."

She shot him a scowl over her shoulder, then snatched the covers over her shoulder and faced the wall again.

"Come on, Sal," he wheedled. "You've got to admit it was pretty funny."

"I think I liked you better before you discovered your sense of humor."

"What's that supposed to mean?"

"You didn't used to laugh. Ever. Nothing was ever funny to you."

He tugged her shoulder, forcing her to face him again. "When was that?"

"Before you had the heart attack! The guys at the office would tell jokes and you never laughed."

"I don't recall anybody ever telling jokes."

"See?" she cried and rolled from the bed. "My point exactly."

"Where are you going?" he called after her.

"To get my cell. I forgot to check my messages."

She stomped across the hall, grabbed her phone and stomped back, punching in the code for her voice mail.

"Who called?" he asked as she climbed back into bed.

She held up a hand to silence him so she could hear the message.

"Hi, Sally. Stacy. Hope you're surviving living with

Captain Friendly. I probably shouldn't bother you with this, but thought I better pass it on, just in case. A lady called this morning asking for Vince. Something Parker. I can't remember her first name. Anyway, she said it was imperative that she speak with Vince right away. I didn't think he'd want me to tell anyone he'd had a heart attack and was at home, so I lied and told her he was out of town."

There was a pause, and Sally could almost see Stacy wringing her hands.

"I know I probably shouldn't dump this on you right now, but I thought I should at least tell you about the call. Just in case the woman's a nut case or something and shows up at Vince's house. Forewarned is fore-armed, as they say. I better get back to work. The phone's ringing off the wall. Call me tomorrow and let me know how things are going. Bye."

She punched the delete button and dropped her hands to her lap.

"Well?" Vince prodded. "Who was it?"

Knowing full well what his reaction would be if she told him what the call was about, she leaned to lay the phone on the bedside table. "Stacy."

He pushed up to an elbow. "Is something wrong at the office?"

"No. Everything's fine."

He crawled over her to switch on the light above the bed. "You're lying. Something's wrong isn't it? Did Mark screw up the Holmes deal?" He slammed a fist against the mattress. "Dammit! I knew I should've run the reports myself. What did he do? Crash the system? Corrupt the files?"

She laid a hand on his arm. "Mark didn't do anything."

"Well, what happened then?"

"Stephanie Parker called."

"Who?"

"Stephanie Parker. The lady whose father served with yours in Vietnam."

He reached to switch off the lamp.

"You need to call her, Vince."

He yanked the covers up over him. "No."

She pushed up to an elbow. "Vince. You have to. If nothing else, you owe it to your father."

He rolled to his side, turning his back to her. "I don't owe him anything."

She knew he was hurting, though the pain was buried so deep he probably was no longer aware of it. Slipping an arm over his waist, she pressed her lips to his shoulder. "Tell me about him, Vince."

"There's nothing to tell."

"Yes, there is. I know about the work he did after he returned to Vietnam."

He tensed. "How do you know about that?"

"I read about him on the Internet."

He jackknifed up. "You did *what?*"

"It's not like I did anything illegal," she said in her defense. "Anyone with a computer and an Internet connection can access the same information."

"Why? What possible reason would you have to dig through my family's past?"

"I was curious. When I first told you about Stephanie calling, you refused to discuss your father." She lifted a shoulder. "So I decided to find out about him on my own."

When he only glared, she laid a hand on his thigh, wanting to make him understand. "Vince—"

He brushed her hand away. "Have I ever asked you about your father? Any of your family?"

"No, but I'd be happy to tell you whatever you want to know."

"I don't want to know because it doesn't matter."

"Of course it does," she argued. "Our families are a part of us. They shaped us into who we are today."

"So if my father was a convict, I'd be in prison today?"

"No," she said in frustration. "But having a convict for a father would certainly have left its mark on you, good or bad."

He slanted her a look. "Since you're such an authority on the human psyche, I take it your father was a psychiatrist."

"I don't have a father."

"Right," he said dryly. "And the next thing you're going to tell me is that you're the product of an immaculate conception."

She drew in a breath, searching for patience. "What I should have said is I don't *know* my father. He abandoned my mother when she was two months pregnant with me."

He grimaced. "Sorry. That had to be tough."

"For my mother. I doubt it's ever easy to raise a child alone. The tough part for me came when my mother died."

"How old were you?"

"Twelve."

"Who took care of you?"

"My grandmother—my mother's mother—took me in. I lived with her until I married."

He gaped. "Married! You never said anything about being married."

She would've laughed at the stricken look on his face, if she hadn't understood the reason behind it. "That's because I no longer am. I've been divorced for over a year."

"You might have mentioned it, you know."

"Why? That's all in the past."

"The same as my father is in my past."

She opened her mouth to argue, then closed it, realizing he had a point. "You're right," she conceded. "I should have told you. If you want, I'll answer any questions you might have."

He held up a hand. "If it's all the same to you, I think I'll pass." Hooking an arm around her waist, he drew her down to lie with him. "I know all I need to know about you."

"You know nothing at all about me."

He rolled to his side and pressed his mouth to hers. "Sure I do. I know you're a damn good secretary." His lips spread across hers in a smile, as he stroked a hand down her hips. "And I know you're hell in bed."

"I'd hardly call that a character reference," she said wryly.

He rested his forehead against her chin and swept his fingers up her inner thigh to cup her mound. "I know you're not an exhibitionist. Your reaction to Pat seeing you naked was proof of that."

Caught in midshiver, she pushed at his head. "Thanks for reminding me of *that* particular humiliation."

Chuckling, he pressed his mouth to hers again. "Remind me tomorrow to have the locks changed on the gates. I don't want you worrying about somebody walking in on us the next time we go skinny-dipping."

"Housekeeper comes today."

Busy emptying the dishwasher, Sally glanced toward the den, where Vince lay stretched out on the sofa. Though she hadn't pursued their conversation the previous evening—Vince had a way of distracting her—his reference to his housekeeper by profession, rather than by name, seemed the perfect opening to bring up the subject again.

"She has a name, you know."

"So?"

"So, why don't you use it instead of referring to her as the housekeeper?"

"What difference does it make what I call her?"

She eyed him suspiciously. "You don't know her name, do you?"

"Sure I do. It's, uh…Maria."

"Mary," she informed him.

He shrugged. "I was close."

Rolling her eyes, she shut the dishwasher door and crossed to the den. "You need to make an effort to get to know the people who work for you."

"Why? I pay them well. That should be enough."

"And I'm sure your employees appreciate your generosity. But while monetary compensation might get the job done, it doesn't necessarily earn you your employees loyalty or respect."

"And me getting to know them will?"

She braced her forearms over the back of the couch. "Doing so creates a relationship. Loyalty grows from that."

He eyed her suspiciously. "Are you sure your father wasn't a psychiatrist?"

Rolling her eyes, she turned away.

He caught her arm and tugged her back. "Don't get in a huff. I was just kidding."

"I was trying to carry on a serious conversation with you," she said in frustration.

He dragged a hand down his face, wiping away his smile. "Sorry. I promise I'll do better."

"Did you know that Mary's son wants to go to college next year?"

He lifted a brow. "Mary has kids?"

She pointed an accusing finger at him. "See? That's exactly what I'm talking about. You don't know anything about the people who work for you."

"Why is it so important that I know Mary has kids?"

"Because they're important to *her*. She's proud of Jesse and she's worried she and her husband won't be able to afford to send him to college."

"There are scholarships available for students with needs."

"And he's applied for several. But what if he isn't

awarded a scholarship? He'll have to go to work and save the money himself, which we both know will delay, maybe even end, his dream of furthering his education."

He stared at her a moment, then shook his head. "If he wants it bad enough, he'll get a degree. Others have done it without any help. Why can't he?"

"I'm sure he'll try. But life sometimes gets in the way of our dreams. He could fall in love and get married or something could happen that forces him to drain his savings. Sickness. A need for transportation. Any number of things could force him to spend the money on something else."

"What's his interest? His field of study?"

She sent up a silent prayer of thanks that she seemed to have finally reached him. "Computers. Mary says he's a true geek. Spends all his time building systems, then taking them apart. He even wrote a software program for his high school that enables the teachers to enter their students' grades into a central database."

"Sharp kid."

"Yes, he is," she agreed. "But just think what he might be capable of with the proper training."

Sally heard the back door open and clamped a hand over Vince's shoulder. "That's Mary now," she warned in a whisper. "Don't tell her I told you about Jesse. She has her pride."

Turning, she opened her arms. "Mary! Hey, it's great to see you again."

Mary bustled into the den and gave Sally a big hug. "What are you doing here? Shouldn't you be at work?"

Sally tipped her head toward the couch. "Doctor ordered Vince home for the week, so I'm working here."

Mary looked at Vince, her face creased with concern. "You're sick?"

He rolled to his feet, as if to prove there was nothing wrong with him. "Just taking an R&R."

Nodding, Mary backed toward the kitchen. "I'll try to stay out of your way and not disturb you."

"I can go outside," he told her. He slid a glance at Sally. "Unless Sally has other plans for me."

His meaning was all to clear and put a blush on her cheeks.

"Not at the moment."

Vince rounded the couch and headed for the patio, but stopped and glanced back at Mary. "By the way, how's Jesse doing?"

Mary glanced at Sally as if surprised by the question. "F-fine. Studying hard for finals."

Nodding, he stepped outside. "That's good. Real good."

Sally watched him, knowing full well it was her conversation with him that had spawned the question. There was a kinder, more compassionate side of Vince, she told herself. It simply needed nurturing in order to grow.

One of these days, if she continued to nurture it along, he might even find enough heart to call Stephanie Parker.

Seven

During the week Sally spent at Vince's house, she tried not to think about "life after the heart attack," which is how she'd come to think of the day she would have to leave his home and return to her own apartment. When the thoughts did slip into her mind, she shoved them out again. In the short time she'd spent with Vince, she'd grown used to living with him, sleeping with him. Granted, the first couple of days had been miserable. But after they'd become lovers, her outlook had changed…as had her sleeping arrangements.

She liked sleeping with Vince and looked forward to cuddling with him at night. Prior to experiencing the phenomenon herself, she would've never dreamed he was such a snuggler, and was pleasantly surprised to discover he seemed to enjoy sleeping close as much as she did. Her ex had hated cuddling and Sally had usually awakened, clinging to the side of the bed, as he preferred to take his half of the middle. After their divorce, one of her biggest thrills was having an entire bed to herself—which made her wonder why she would miss sleeping with Vince.

But miss him she would.

Her only consolation was that she would continue to see him at work, and it was on that lone bright spot she made herself focus as she packed her bag Sunday morning, preparing for her departure.

"Sally?"

"In here!" she called, as she tucked her bikini into her suitcase.

"What are you doing?"

She glanced over her shoulder to find Vince standing in the doorway. "Packing." Though she felt more like crying, she forced a bright smile. "Your days with Nurse Ratchett are over. It's Sunday and time for me to head home."

"No."

She blinked. "Excuse me?"

He strode across the room, grabbed her bag and marched across the hall with it to his bedroom.

Sally ran after him. "Give that back! I'm not done packing."

Ignoring her, he opened the suitcase over his bed, dumping its contents onto the silk spread, then tossed it to the floor and faced her. "Just because it's Sunday doesn't mean you have to go. You're staying right here."

Though "here" was exactly where Sally wanted to stay, she didn't care for his tone or his domineering attitude.

Snatching up her bag, she began cramming her clothes back inside.

"I agreed to stay a week," she informed him. "That week is officially over and I'm going home."

He grabbed the bag, and a tug-of-war ensued, with each stubbornly pulling in opposite directions. Frustrated, Sally released her hold, and Vince stumbled back, hugging the bag to his chest.

"Why are you doing this?" she cried. "You don't need me to take care of you any longer."

"Says who?"

"Your doctor. *Me*. To be honest, you didn't need me past the first twenty-four hours. You're more than—"

"I don't want you to go."

"—capable of…" She blinked. "What did you say?"

"I don't want you to go."

She stared, telling herself not to put too much hope into what he was saying. "You don't?"

"No." He tossed the suitcase to the bed. "You could stay, couldn't you? It's not like you have anyone waiting for you at your apartment."

"Well, no," she said hesitantly. "I don't."

"Then why not stay here?" He strode to the closet and grabbed up an armload of his clothing. "There's plenty of room for you to hang your things," he said as he dumped the clothes over a chair. He returned to the closet and began pulling shoes off the rack and pitching them to the floor. "Shoes, too," he added.

Her heart melting, she laid a hand on his arm. "Vince, stop. There's no need for you to destroy your closet. I don't have that many clothes."

The shoe he held slipped from his hand. "Are you saying you'll stay?"

"Yes."

With a whoop, he grabbed her up and spun her in a dizzying circle.

Laughing, she pushed at his shoulders. "Put me down, before you drop me."

"I won't drop you." To prove it, he shifted her over his shoulder in a fireman's carry and headed out of the closet.

"Vince!" she cried laughing. "Put me down."

"Okay."

He dumped her onto to the bed, then dived over her. Buried beneath him, she struggled to breathe. "Get off me," she choked out.

"Put me down," he mimicked. "Get off me." Bracing his hands on the bed, he pushed up to look down at her. "You're mighty damn hard to please."

She reached up to place a hand against his cheek. "You're the one who wanted me to stay."

"I did, didn't I?" Heavy a weary sigh, he rolled off her and dragged her hand over to clasp over his heart. "Guess I'm stuck with you now."

If not for the warmth in the eyes that gazed at her, she might've been offended.

Lacing her fingers through his, she snuggled close. "Looks like it."

Sally and Vince's first argument as new roommates took place in the garage the next morning prior to work. Vince wanted Sally to ride with him, but Sally stubbornly insisted upon taking her own car. Her reasoning was justifiable—to her mind, at least. She thought it best if they kept their living arrangement a secret from her coworkers, and knew that arriving in the same car with Vince would spawn a flood of gossip and speculation regarding their relationship.

Vince finally gave in and let her take her car, though he made it clear he thought it ridiculous, when they were going to the same place.

After having missed a week of work, Sally's desk was piled high with mail and phone calls to return. Her duties kept her chained to her desk, while Vince spent most of his day away from his, tied up in meetings with department heads scattered throughout the building.

Around three he passed through her office on the way to his. Engrossed in a spreadsheet, Sally didn't even look up.

Moments later her intercom buzzed. "Yes?" she said.

"I need to see you in my office."

"Can it wait a second?" she asked hopefully. "I only have two pages to finish for the inventory updates on the Jones account."

"No it can't."

Surprised by the impatience in his voice, she grabbed

a pad and headed for his office. "Is there a—" She stopped and frowned, when she didn't find him sitting at his desk.

The door slammed behind her and she whirled, a squeal building in her throat. Before she could release it, Vince smothered her mouth with his. She darted a nervous glance over his shoulder at the door that separated her office from his, praying no one happened by, then wrapped her arms around him and melted against him. She tasted the impatience in him, the need, and answered it with her own.

Dragging his mouth from hers, he released a husky sigh. "Damn. I've been wanting to do that all day."

Pleased that she'd been on his mind, she dragged a nail down the front of his shirt. "I thought you were in meetings all day?"

"I was." He stroked a hand down her back. "Couldn't concentrate for thinking about you."

"Careful," she warned. "I hear the boss is tough on slackers."

"Yeah, I've heard that rumor, too."

Her nail slid down his fly and, with a groan, he turned her back to the door and pinned her arms above her head. Burying his face in the curve of her neck, he dragged in a deep, shuddery breath. "How soon do you think we can get out of here?"

"Vince!" she cried, laughing. "It's not even three o'clock."

He pushed a knee between her thighs. "And your point is?"

She melted against him, then snapped up her head. "Did you hear that?" she whispered.

He nipped at her earlobe. "Hear what?"

"*That!* Somebody's in my office." She struggled to free her hands. "Let me go. I don't want anybody catching us like this."

He released her, watching as she smoothed her hair into place and adjusted her blouse.

"Do I look all right?" she asked him nervously.

"Any better and I'd throw you down on the floor right here and now."

She sputtered a laugh, then quickly sobered, fearing the sound might carry to the other room. With a last comb of fingers through her hair, she opened the door to find Stacy, her friend and the company's receptionist standing by her desk.

"Stacy," she said, feigning surprise, then called over her shoulder to Vince, "I'll take care of that right away," and closed the door behind her. "What brings you to the executive floor?" she asked Stacy as she crossed to her desk.

Stacy shot a glance toward Vince's office, then whispered, "You got a call a few minutes ago."

Puzzled by Stacy's cloak-and-dagger act, Sally sat down behind her desk. "From whom?"

"A man," Stacy whispered, then lifted a brow, as if that explained everything.

Sally sputtered a laugh. "So? I get calls from men all the time."

"Not personal ones."

A sliver of dread skated down Sally's spine.

"Did he leave a message?"

"I connected him to your voice mail, but I have no way of knowing whether he left one or not."

Sally struggled to keep the dread from her face. "Well, whoever he is, he'll have to wait. Right now I've got a report to finish."

"He's called before," Stacy went on. "At least twice last week while you were at Vince's. I told him you were out of the office for the week, and offered to connect him to your voice mail, but he hung up before I could."

Sally shook her head sadly. "I swear. People can be so rude. I'm sorry you were subjected to that kind of behavior."

"I've dealt with worse."

When Stacy made no move to leave, Sally looked at her curiously. "Was there something else?"

"No, that was it." She gave Vince's door another glance, then sidled closer to the desk and said in a low voice, "I'm dying to hear about your week with Captain Friendly. All the girls are."

Sally slipped her hand to her lap and crossed her fingers. "Nothing much to tell," she lied. "Pretty boring, if you want to know the truth. We played some board games. Swam some." She lifted a shoulder. "That's about it."

Stacy's eyes bugged. "You went swimming with Captain Friendly?"

"It was no big deal," she said, trying to make light of what had to have been the sensual experience of her life. "Since his doctor wouldn't allow him to watch television or work, there was very little left for us to do."

"Man," Stacy said, releasing a pent-up breath. "I can't imagine being trapped in the same room with him for more than five minutes, much less a whole week. You've got to be a saint to have put up with a grouch like him."

Oh, if only you knew, Sally thought, but shrugged again. "It wasn't so bad."

Stacy glanced at her watch and wrinkled her nose. "I better get back to the switchboard. Helen's manning it for me and I promised I wouldn't be gone long."

Not wanting to give Stacy an excuse to linger, Sally shifted her chair before her computer screen. "Thanks for letting me know about the phone call, Stace. I appreciate the heads-up."

"No problem."

She waited until Stacy was out of earshot, then picked up her phone and quickly punched in her code to retrieve her voice mail. Holding the phone to her ear, she closed her eyes, willing the voice she heard to be anyone other than the one she feared.

"Where the hell are you, Sally? And why aren't you returning my calls?"

She quickly replaced the receiver, not wanting to hear any more, then covered her face with her hands.

Please, God, she prayed silently. *Don't let him do something stupid and mess this up for me. I've paid a big enough price for my mistakes. Surely I shouldn't have to suffer anymore.*

"Sally?"

She dropped her hands at the sound of Vince's voice and glanced over her shoulder. "What?"

"Is something wrong?"

Wrinkling her forehead, she rubbed at the crease between her eyes. "Just a little headache. Probably from staring at the computer screen all day."

"Why don't you cut out early? You look like you could use the break."

She slanted a guilty look at the stack of work piled on her desk, wanting to take him up on his offer, but knowing if she did she'd just be that much further behind tomorrow. "No. I really should finish updating the inventory for the Jones account."

His hands lit on her shoulders and squeezed. "It'll wait. Go on home and put your feet up for a while." He pressed a kiss to the top of her head. "And don't worry about dinner. I'll pick us up something on the way home."

Touched by his thoughtfulness, she laid her hand over his. "Thanks, Vince. I appreciate this more than you know."

Vince left the office later than he'd planned, delayed by a call from a broker in California who was looking for a buyer for a food chain. He did remember his promise to Sally, though, and stopped by his favorite Chinese restaurant, leaving with enough food to feed a small army. Since he wasn't sure what her tastes were, he'd selected a variety of dishes, hoping he'd score on at least one.

As he made the drive home, he found his thoughts drifting to Sally—which in itself was an oddity, as business usually dominated his thoughts. When he'd walked out of his office and seen her sitting at her desk with her hands covering her face, for a moment he'd thought she was crying. Yet, when she'd turned to look at him, he'd seen no sign of tears. She had looked pale, though. When he'd questioned her, she'd claimed she had a headache. He supposed that could be true, but something told him it was something else entirely. She certainly hadn't seemed to be suffering from a headache when he'd been kissing her in his office only moments before.

But why would she lie?

Shaking off the puzzling thoughts, he turned onto his street, anxious to get home. He passed a car parked on the side of the street and gave it a cursory glance, before turning onto his driveway. He noticed Sally's car parked in front of one of the garage stalls and made a mental note to give her a remote control, so she could park inside.

After gathering the bags of take-out from the passenger seat, he climbed from his car and reached to punch the button to lower the garage door. Hearing voices outside, he dropped his hand and walked out to the driveway to look around. Due to the size of the lots in River Oaks, he rarely, if ever, heard any kind of noise from his neighbors, thus his concern.

He paused to listen and was sure the voices were coming from the far side of his house. Prepared to give whoever was trespassing on his property a piece of his mind, he set his jaw and strode in that direction.

What—or rather who—he found there, stopped him in his tracks.

A man had Sally by the arm, while gesturing wildly with the other. Without a thought for his own safety,

Vince dropped the sacks of take-out and charged, vising his arms around the man's chest from behind and jerking him back.

An elbow rammed his stomach, knocking the breath from him and loosening his grip. Finding himself facing Sally's attacker, he lowered his head like a bull and rammed his head into the guy's midsection and took him down. Moving quickly, he straddled him and closed a hand over the man's throat. The smell of liquor on the man's breath was strong, the eyes that glared at him bloodshot. "You okay?" he gasped.

Though Vince's gaze was fixed on the man's face, his question was for Sally.

"I…I'm fine."

Keeping his hand on the man's throat, he used the other to unclip his cell from his belt and tossed it to Sally. "Call the police."

When she didn't move, he said more sharply, "Call the police, dammit! I can't hold him here forever."

Gulping, she tucked the phone behind her back. "Let him go, Vince."

"What? Are you crazy? He was going to hit you."

"Let him go, Vince. Please." She shifted her gaze to the man on the ground and narrowed her eyes. "You'll leave, won't you, Brad? Tell him you'll leave if he'll let you up."

"Bitch," the guy she'd called Brad all but spat at her. "Not without my money."

"*Your* money?" she cried. "*You* don't have any money. Not anymore."

"Because you stole it."

"I did no such thing. When I left, I took only what was mine."

Vince looked from Sally to the man he sat on, then back at Sally. "This guy's your husband?" he asked incredulously.

"*Ex*-husband," she corrected.

Vince looked down at the man again. "And you say she has your money?"

"I don't have anything of his!" Sally cried.

Vince hauled in a breath and slowly released it, fighting for patience while he tried to make sense out of what was quickly turning out to be nightmare. "Maybe it would be better if you went inside and let me handle this, Sally."

She folded her arms across her chest. "I'm not going anywhere."

He narrowed an eye at her. "Sally. Go inside."

She hesitated a moment, as if she intended to refuse again, then spun on her heel and strode away.

Vince waited until he heard the front door slam behind her, then turned his gaze on her ex again. "Now. Back to the original question. You say she has you money?"

"Damn right. Ten thousand dollars."

"And what makes you think she has it?"

"Because it's gone."

Which only proved what Vince had suspected. From what he could see, the guy was a loser, a drunk. If he'd truly ever had ten thousand dollars, Vince would bet everything he owned the guy had pissed it away on booze.

"Sally doesn't lie," he informed her ex. "Which makes me believe her story and not yours."

Brad curled his lip in a sneer. "You're sleeping with her, aren't you? You think I don't know what's been going on between the two of you? I've been watching your house for days. She's got you whipped, buddy. Sashaying that sweet little ass of hers in your face, while leading you around by the nose."

The fury that burned through Vince was unlike any he'd ever experienced before. He tightened his fingers around Brad's neck until the man's eyes bulged. Fearing he'd kill him if he remained any longer, he pushed to his feet and leveled a finger at Brad's nose. "If I ever see you anywhere near Sally or hear that you've harassed her in any way, I'll hunt you down like the dog you are and beat the living hell out of you. Understand?"

Scowling, Brad rubbed a hand over the band of red Vince had left on his neck, then rolled to his knees. He knelt there a moment, his head hanging between his arms, then hitched himself to his feet. Weaving drunkenly, he started for his car.

"She's after your money," he said to Vince. "Wait and see. She'll bleed you dry the same as she did me."

Sally stood in front of the wall of windows that looked out over the back lawn, rubbing her hands up and down her arms. She was furious, humiliated. Why had Brad come here of all places? she cried silently. And how on earth had he found out where Vince lived? Vince guarded his privacy as diligently as soldiers did Fort

Knox. His phone number was unlisted and he was careful about who he gave out information to.

But somehow Brad had managed to find his house, as well as Sally.

Tears welled in her eyes, as humiliation burned through her again. For Vince to see Brad that way and know that she'd once been married to him embarrassed her as much as it shamed her. Sloppy drunk, his clothes dirty, his face unshaven, his breath reeking of cheap whiskey. It sickened her to see how far Brad had fallen from the man she'd once loved and married.

She heard the mud room door open and tensed, knowing it was Vince coming inside. Unable to bear facing him, she remained before the window, her arms hugged around her middle, staring out.

His footsteps sounded behind her and she swallowed back the emotion that clotted her throat. "Is he gone?"

"Yeah."

She felt the weight of his hand on her shoulder, the warmth of his breath against the back of her neck and closed her eyes to squeeze back the tears. "I don't have his money. I swear I don't."

He rubbed a hand over her shoulder. "I never thought you did."

"Oh, God," she cried, and covered her face with her hands. "I'm so sorry he came here. That you saw him like that."

"Hey," he soothed, turning her into his arms. "There's no need to cry. He's gone now. He won't ever bother you again."

Refusing to be comforted, she shook her head. "He'll be back. No matter how hard I try to escape him, he always manages to find me."

He drew back and lifted her chin, forcing her gaze to his. "He's done this before?"

She gulped, nodded. "When he's broke. He always promises to pay me back, but he never does."

"Does he really believe you took ten thousand dollars of his?"

Dropping her gaze, she lifted a shoulder. "I don't know. Probably, although that's new." She looked up at him, his face blurred by the tears that filled her eyes. "It's the liquor. It has to be. He's become delusional. Thinks everybody is out to get him."

"Obviously."

She shook her head, desperate to make him understand. "He wasn't always like that. He was a football player. A good one. The pros spotted him while he was still in high school and followed him to college, promising him a contract when he graduated."

"They reneged on the offer?"

She shook her head again. "He got hurt. Senior year of college. He was a quarterback. Dropped back to make a pass. A tackle clipped him just below the knees. Shattered his femur. Ripped the ligaments in his knees. He knew his career was over before the ambulance left the field with him."

"Tough break."

She sniffed, nodded. "Yeah, it was." She turned her face to the window, remembering the horror of that day and those that followed. "We'd only been married a little over a year. I had dropped out of college to support us, so he could continue to play football. He'd placed all his dreams and based our future on making the pros. Losing that dream destroyed him.

"He was used to being in the limelight. Seeing his name in the paper all the time. Having strangers come up to him and ask for his autograph. He was a hero. A star. Once it was announced that he'd never play again, that light faded quickly. He was a has-been. In his eyes, a failure."

She shook her head sadly. "He didn't know how to deal with being average, refused to accept the fact that he was no longer a star. He started drinking. Staying out until all hours of the night. Sometimes not bothering to come home at all." She shuddered, remembering the fear, the embarrassment, worse, the debts he incurred. "He couldn't keep a job. Would never admit it was his own fault he kept getting fired. It was always someone else's fault. Never his."

"And you stuck with him?"

She closed her eyes, the guilt she'd carried the day she'd left him weighing on her as strongly as it had then. Opening her eyes, she turned to face him again. "How could I leave him? He was my husband. I loved him. I couldn't just walk away and let him drink himself to death."

His gaze on hers, he lifted a hand to her cheek and stroked his thumb beneath her eye. "You blame yourself."

It was a statement, not a question. Embarrassed by

what she considered a weakness, she dropped her gaze. "Sometimes. Back then, all the time. I know it wasn't my fault." She tapped a finger against her head. "Up here, I do. I've sat through enough AA sessions to know I wasn't to blame. Brad was the one with the problem. Not me." She fisted a hand against her chest. "But sometimes my heart wants me to believe something different. When I see what he's become, how far he's fallen from the man I once knew, I feel as if there was something I could have done to stop him, to *fix* him. To make him better."

He brought her fist to his lips and pressed a kiss against her knuckles. "You can't fix him, Sal. Nobody can. He has to fix himself."

Touched by his reassurance, his tenderness, she laid her cheek against his chest and released a last shuddery breath. "I needed to hear that. Even though I know better, every time I see him, all the guilt comes rushing back." Drawing in a shuddery breath, she lifted her head and smiled at him. "Thanks."

He gave her bottom a pat. "You're welcome." Releasing her, he turned for the kitchen. "Hungry? I brought home Chinese."

She pressed a hand against her heart as she watched him walk away, stunned by the ease and his obvious willingness to put the event behind them. He'd just lived her greatest nightmare, discovered her deepest and darkest secret. She'd thought for sure he'd send her packing. Instead he wanted to eat Chinese food with her?

If she wasn't already a bit in love with him, this would have cinched it for sure.

Convinced there was hope for Vince yet—and possibly a future for them—she started for the kitchen. "Starving. I hope you got egg rolls."

Eight

The phone rang. After living without one in the house for a week, Sally jolted at the unexpected sound.

"Would you mind getting that?" Vince called from the bathroom. "I've got shaving cream all over my hands."

"Sure." She flopped to her stomach and stretched to pluck the receiver from the base on the bedside table. "Donnelly residence."

"Mrs. Donnelly?"

"No, this is—" She was about to say "his secretary" but thought better of it and said simply "—Sally. May I ask who is calling?"

"Wade Parker. My wife Stephanie has been trying to get in touch with Mr. Donnelly for a couple of weeks now."

Sally's eyes shot wide at the name Parker. "Just a minute and I'll see if Vince is available." Punching the mute button, she rolled from the bed and ran for the bathroom. Her heart beating like a drum against her chest, she held out the phone to Vince. "It's for you."

He cut his gaze to hers in the bathroom mirror. "Who is it?"

"Wade Parker."

He tipped up his chin and resumed shaving. "Don't know him."

"He's Stephanie's husband. You know. The lady whose dad served with yours in Vietnam."

He lowered his razor and held it beneath the faucet. "Tell him I'm not here."

She thrust the phone at him. "I'm not going to lie for you."

"Then tell him I'm not interested." He picked up an end of the towel that draped his neck and wiped it across his face. "That isn't a lie. I'm not."

"Vince, please," she begged. "At least talk to him. Hear what he has to say."

He stripped the towel from around his neck and dropped it to the floor as he stepped into the shower. His emphatic "No" was followed by the *thunk* of the door shower closing behind him.

Her shoulders drooping in disappointment, Sally punched the mute button again to disengage the feature and lifted the phone to her ear. "I'm sorry," she said and told the lie she'd sworn she wouldn't tell for Vince. "Mr. Donnelly is unable to come to the phone right now."

"Maybe you can help me."

She glanced at the steam that misted the shower door, then backed into the bedroom, pulling the bathroom closed behind her. "I'm not sure I can," she said uneasily.

She listened while he explained his wife's frustration in trying to contact Vince, and totally sympathized with the woman, because Sally was pretty frustrated with him, too. Her eyes widened in fascination as he began to tell the story behind the missing piece of paper, the pieces already found and shared with her the desire of those who held pieces of the document to locate the remaining missing ones, emphasizing their interest wasn't in the value it might hold when joined, but the sentimental value it held.

"Wow," Sally murmured, totally engrossed by the tale. "Do you really think the document's valuable?"

"We won't know that until all the pieces are located. If you could persuade Mr. Donnelly to cooperate with us, it would increase our chances. At the moment we've hit a wall in our efforts to track down the remaining soldiers. Vince is our only hope at the moment."

"I don't know," she said doubtfully, and glanced at the bathroom door. "Vince refuses to talk about his father."

"Surely there's a way to persuade him to help us. If it's money he wants, I'm willing to negotiate with him on a fair price."

Sally had to swallow a laugh. "Vince can't be seduced by money. He's got plenty of his own."

A weary sigh crossed the line, then Mr. Parker said, "Well, we'd appreciate whatever help you can give us.

My wife's about to drive me crazy over this. It means a lot to her and, to be honest, I've gotten caught up in the mystery myself."

"Yeah," Sally said. "I share your pain."

She heard the water shut off in the bathroom and said quickly, "I have to go, Mr. Parker. I'll do my best to help you."

"Couldn't ask more of a person than that. Thank you."

She quickly replaced the receiver and slid beneath the covers. They'd barely had time to settle over her stomach, when the bathroom door opened and Vince walked out, wearing a towel.

"All clean?" she asked and prayed she didn't look as guilty as she felt.

He stripped the towel from around his waist and scrubbed it over his wet hair as he crossed to the bed. "Yep. Even washed behind my ears."

Finding it difficult to keep her gaze from trailing down his mouth-watering physique, she scooted to the edge of the bed. "Let me see."

He dipped his head down, as if to allow her to check behind his ears, but hooked the towel around her neck instead and drew her face to his. "Gotcha."

Smiling, she wound her arms around his neck. "Doesn't count. I wanted to be caught."

"Ah, now you've gone and taken all the fun out of seducing you." Burying a knee in the mattress, he pressed his mouth to hers and forced her back to the bed. "But I'll see if I can work up some enthusiasm for the job." He stroked a hand down her side, then brought it up the inside of her leg, his touch light as a feather.

"Mmm," she hummed, with a delicious shiver. "Working for me. How about you?"

He parted her legs and pushed a knuckle down her fold. "Getting there."

The knuckle dipped into her center and her hips bucked instinctively.

His lips curved in a smile. "Believe I'm there."

Though Sally didn't mention her conversation with Wade Parker to Vince, it remained on her mind. She knew it wasn't going to be easy to persuade Vince to talk to the Parkers, and she wanted to wait for the appropriate time to bring up the subject.

The opening she needed presented itself the following weekend and in a very unexpected way.

She was curled up beside Vince on the sofa, waiting patiently while he surfed the channels in search of a program for them to watch. The choices were slim on a normal Saturday night, but on this particular night they seemed worse than usual.

"Everything is a rerun," she complained.

"That wrestling match we were watching wasn't a rerun."

She rolled her eyes. "That stuff is so fake. Do you really think that guy would still have been standing if the chair his opponent cracked over his head was real wood?"

"Maybe he has a thick skull."

She rapped her knuckles against Vince's head. "Like yours?"

"Funny."

She flapped a hand at the TV. "Try the Movie Channel. Maybe they're showing something we haven't seen."

Vince scrolled down the guide until he reached the channel, punched Select, then settled back, draping an arm over Sally's shoulders.

A commercial was currently playing. At its end, the screen segued to what appeared to be a war scene. Soldiers lay on their stomachs in tall grass, while bombs exploded in the sky overhead.

"Hell no," Vince said, and aimed the remote at the TV.

Sally caught his arm. "No, wait. I think this is that Mel Gibson movie *We Were Soldiers*. I haven't seen it. Have you?"

"No, and I don't partiularly care to watch it now."

"Please, Vince?" she begged. "I've had a crush on Mel Gibson ever since the first *Lethal Weapon* came out."

Grimacing, he slouched down on the couch and passed her the control. "Fine. Watch it. I'm taking a nap."

Sally made sure it was impossible for him to sleep. Every so often, she'd increase the volume a notch or two. With the fancy sound system he had hooked up to his TV, it was if the war was being fought all around them.

After a rather intense combat scene, she stole a look at Vince and was pleased to see that he was not only awake, but had his gaze riveted on the screen.

By the end of the movie, Sally had soaked two tissues and was working on a third.

She pressed a hand to her chest. "Oh, my gosh," she said, then gulped a steadying breath. "That was the best movie I've seen in ages. And so realistic." She turned to peer at Vince. "Can you imagine what it must have been like to be one of those soldiers? Or worse, one of the wives waiting back home?" She shuddered just thinking about it. "I don't know how they stood it. Living day to day, never knowing if your husband was alive or dead, fearing the next knock on the door would be a chaplain coming to give you the news your husband was killed in battle?" She dabbed the tissue at her eyes. "I don't think I would have survived."

Vince snatched the remote from her hand and punched the power button. The screen went black, throwing the room into darkness.

"You'd have survived," he muttered.

She pressed her head back against the cushion and stared at the ceiling high overhead. "I don't know that I would."

"You survived a divorce, didn't you?"

"Yes, but that was a choice I made. Those women didn't *choose* to lose their husbands. Each and every one of them wanted her husband to come home alive."

"Marry a soldier and you're taking the chance he's going to die. Especially during wartime."

She rolled her head to the side to look at him. "Were you old enough to remember when your father was in Vietnam?"

"No. I was a baby."

She reached to lace her fingers through his. "That must have been really hard on your mother. Having her husband so far away and her alone with a baby to take care of."

"Him coming home didn't change anything. She was still alone."

Hearing the bitterness in his voice, she gave his hand a reassuring squeeze. "You resented the time he spent away."

"Damn right. He was out taking care of everybody else and ignoring his responsibilities to his own family."

"He was never home?"

She felt his shoulder lift in a shrug against hers.

"He was there some. Never long, though. People were always calling him. Some soldier who needed counseling or a widow who was being evicted because she couldn't pay the rent."

"He helped so many," she said softly. "Surely you must be proud of the work he did."

"Oh, I'm proud all right," he said wryly. "I was downright overjoyed the night I graduated from high school and he was off sobering up a drunk, instead of sitting in the auditorium watching me get my degree. And I was ecstatic the day I rode in the back seat of a cab with my mom, after she'd had a miscarriage, while some stranger drove us to the hospital. Yeah, my dad was a hero, all right. To everybody but his own damn family," he added bitterly.

Sally reached to comb his hair back from his face. "Have you ever talked to anybody about how you feel?"

He glanced her way, as if to see if she was serious,

and scowled when he saw that she was. "I don't need a psychiatrist. What I needed was my dad."

"I wasn't suggesting that you needed a psychiatrist. Talking sometimes helps. Especially if you can to talk to someone who's shared the same experiences." Taking a chance, she leaned over and pressed a kiss to his cheek. "Why don't you call Stephanie Parker? Her father served with yours. There's a chance she's experienced the same resentment as you. Talking to her might help you understand your father better. Maybe even help you find it in your heart to forgive him."

He bolted from the couch, knocking her arm away. "I don't need to talk to anyone about my father," he said angrily, then pointed a finger at her nose. "And that includes you. If he'd died in Vietnam, I'd have been better off. My mother would've been, too."

She sat up, her eyes wide in horror. "Vince, you don't mean that."

"I damn sure do. If he'd died there, my mother would have grieved, sure, but she would have eventually picked up the pieces of her life and gone on. Maybe even married again. Who knows what she would've done. Instead she was forced to make do with what little was left after he'd given his money, *our* money, to others he thought had a greater need. And she wouldn't have lain in bed at night crying because she missed him, wishing he was home with her instead of sitting in some hospital holding the hand of vet who was dying from the effects of Agent Orange. She wouldn't have had to—"

He cut himself off in midsentence and flapped a

hand. "I don't know why the hell I'm wasting my breath telling you all this. If I talked all night, I'd never be able to make you understand what it was like."

"You could try," she offered quietly.

"Why? Talking about it won't change a damn thing." He turned away. "I'm going to bed. If you want to sleep with me, fine. If you don't, that's fine, too."

Sally lay beside Vince, her chest aching as if it had suffered a mortal blow. Her nerves trembled beneath her skin. Her eyes burned with unshed tears. Her heart felt as if was breaking in two.

While she lay there, the things Vince had said played over and over through her mind in an unending litany of despair and doom. He was filled with such resentment, such bitterness over the injustices he felt he'd suffered at his father's hand that it was a wonder he'd made it this far in life without suffering a meltdown.

After listening to the brief glimpses he'd shared of his life, she could understand why he might feel the way he did. But that didn't mean she thought how he'd chosen to handle his feelings was right. It wasn't healthy for a person to hold all that hatred inside. Doing so was bound to effect his personality, his beliefs, destroy any chance of happiness.

In Vince's case, it already had.

Hadn't she seen proof of his selfishness displayed in a thousand different ways during the months she'd worked as his secretary? Witnessed his indifference to the people who worked for him?

She squeezed her eyes shut, hearing again his last words to her.

If you want to sleep with me, fine. If you don't, that's fine, too.

When he said the words, the cold indifference in his voice had sent a chill down her spine, and it did now as she remembered them. She'd told herself he hadn't meant to hurt her. That it was the anger talking, not Vince. He wasn't that cruel. He couldn't be. Clinging to that belief, she'd given him time to calm down before going to his bedroom.

She glanced over to where he lay sleeping, his back turned to her. He hadn't said a word when she'd climbed into bed beside him. And when she'd reached out to lay a hand on his shoulder, he'd shrugged it off.

He didn't care about her, she realized, and felt the fissure in her heart widen. He was selfish and mean-spirited, just as she'd believed him to be before she'd spent the week at his house. He didn't care about her, or anyone, for that matter. Vince Donnelly cared only for himself.

She sank her teeth into her lower lip to force back the sob that threatened. She couldn't stay. No matter how much she thought herself in love with him, she couldn't live with him any longer. She'd lived with a selfish man before, and his selfishness had nearly broken her spirit, beaten her down into believing she was worthless, responsible for his problems, for every bad thing that had ever happened to him in life.

Even knowing that, she still found it hard to turn her

face away from the sight of Vince, even harder to slip from his bed.

And later, when she closed the door of his house behind her and heard the solid click of the lock falling into place, the sound echoed through her body, matching that of her heart breaking.

Nine

Finding himself alone in bed the next morning, Vince stumbled into the bathroom to relieve himself, then went in search of Sally. He felt a niggle of guilt for the way he'd treated her the night before, the anger he'd let spill over onto her. He quickly disposed of it by telling himself she'd deserved whatever anger had landed on her. Hadn't he warned her? He'd told her repeatedly that he didn't want to talk about his father. Any mention of that period of his life opened a long-festering wound, spilling its poison over whoever happened to be near by.

Expecting the smell of coffee to greet him before he reached the kitchen—and disappointed that it hadn't—he called, "Sally? Where are you?"

On the off chance that his nose wasn't working, he continued on to the kitchen and was somewhat relieved to discover his nose was working, as the carafe was empty and apparently hadn't been put to use yet that morning.

Thinking she might be on the patio soaking up sun, an activity that seemed to give her immeasurable pleasure, he pushed open the door and stepped outside. Bright sunlight hit his eyes nearly blinding him and he threw up a hand to shade them as he looked around. Not seeing a sign of Sally, he stepped back inside.

"Sally!" he shouted, as he went from room to room in search of her. "Where the hell are you? I'm hungry."

In the guest room, the bedroom Sally had occupied before moving into his, he found a letter lying on the bed. Dread knotted his gut as he stared at it, unable to bring himself to touch it.

She was gone. He knew it without having to read whatever words she'd written, felt the pain of it sear clear through his bones. Why? he thought silently. Why would she leave like this without telling him, without so much as a word of explanation?

The answer hit him hard, nearly dragging him to his knees.

He was the cause. As sure as if he'd shoved her out the door himself, he was the reason she was gone. His anger, his bitterness. His refusal to talk about his father. His stubborn defiance in not returning the Parker woman's call.

He dropped down on the side of the bed and dragged the letter closer, needing to touch it, needing the proof that she was really gone. Her scent drifted up from the paper—or the bed, he wasn't sure which, as her scent lingered in every room of his house—and filled his mind with images of her. Floating on the raft in the pool, her body lax as she lazily dragged a finger through the water. Laughing and taunting him, when they'd played kick ball on his lawn. Sitting opposite him at the breakfast table, her chin propped on the back of her hands, her eyes sparkling with amusement as she watched him gag down some of the fruit and yogurt she seemed to think he needed.

Dragging in a fortifying breath, he picked up the piece of paper and begin to read:

Vince,

I'm sorry I left without saying goodbye. If you hadn't noticed before, I'm sure you know now that I'm a coward. Leaving is hard for me and I thought I'd save us both the embarrassment of my emotions by leaving while you were asleep.

I truly appreciate the generosity you've shown me as my employer. Few companies pay the kind of salary you offer, and believe me when I say I needed the money. It went a long way in helping me pay off the debts Brad left with me when we divorced. For that alone, I owe you my gratitude.

You'll probably think me ridiculous for even mentioning this, but I thank you, too, for allowing me to house-sit for you when you were out of town. It was a pleasure to stay in such a beautiful home—although I honestly think you should consider finding a new interior decorator. The chrome and black is depressing, as is the art.

He had to stop and drag a hand across his face before he could read on.

I hope you'll forgive me for not giving you the two-week notice you deserve as my employer. As I said before, leaving is hard for me, and this is the only way I thought I could pull this off with any dignity.

I hope you'll remember the changes Dr. O'Connor requested you make in your lifestyle. Cut back on the work, reduce the stress, eat healthier, exercise more. I'd like to add one more item to his list. Smile. You'll be amazed the effect that alone will make in your life.

Take care of yourself, Vince. You'll forever be in my thoughts.

Sally

Vince lifted the letter to his face and breathed in her scent, then clutched the paper against his heart like a bandage, in hopes it could somehow lessen the pain.

It didn't help.

He doubted anything could.

Smile, she'd said. How was he supposed to smile without her there to tease his lips into the shape?

He loved her. He didn't know why he hadn't realized that before now. Losing her was like waking to darkness.

She'd become important to him, a part of him. In the span of a week, she'd settled into his mind and heart as solidly as if he'd known her all his life.

He considered going after her. He didn't have a clue where she lived, but he knew he could find the information in the employment records at his office.

And isn't that pitiful? he told himself. She worked for him, took care of nearly every detail of his life, had lived with him, shared his bed and he didn't even know where the hell she lived.

He supposed it just proved she was right about him. He didn't care enough about his employees to develop a relationship with them. Not even a superficial one, in which he'd at least have learned their addresses.

No, he told himself and carefully folded the letter. He wouldn't go after her. She deserved to be happy.

And Vince Donnelly, in spite of the wealth he'd accrued, lacked the means to give her what she needed, what she deserved.

"Good morning, Stacy."

Stacy snapped up her head at the greeting. "Excuse me?"

Vince couldn't blame his receptionist for looking so surprised. Stacy had worked for him for… Well, he didn't know how long she'd worked for him, but whatever the length of time, he couldn't remember once ever speaking to her when he'd walked past the front desk.

"I said, good morning."

"Oh." She forced a weak smile. "Good morning to you, too, Mr. Donnelly."

It's a start, Vince told himself as he stepped onto the elevator that would take him to the executive floor and his private office. A rough one, but a start. He'd probably never develop the level of heart Sally had wanted from him, but at least he was trying.

Though he knew Sally was gone, he wasn't prepared for the sense of disappointment that hit him when he stepped into her office and didn't find her sitting behind her desk. It wedged in his throat like a rock, threatening to choke him.

Turning his face away, he forced himself to walk past the empty desk, and shut his door behind him, blocking the sight, as well as the reminder that she was gone.

Sally pulled her mail from her box and thumbed through it as she walked back to her apartment. *Bill. Bill. Sales flyer.* She stopped short, her gaze freezing on the return address of the last envelope in the stack. "Donnelly Consulting, 44400 Donnelly Towers, Houston, TX."

Holding a hand against her heart for fear it would beat out of her chest, she ran the remaining distance to her apartment. Once inside, she dropped the rest of the mail on the floor, then sank down on the sofa and held the envelope between trembling hands. She swallowed hard, building her courage, before running her thumb beneath the seal and drawing out the letter enclosed. A handwritten note was paper clipped to the top left corner.

She tugged it free and read:

I thought you might need this when you apply for a new job.

It was signed with the familiar, if barely recognizable V. She gave her chest a bolstering pat before unfolding the letter to read:

To whom it may concern:
    Sally Gregg was employed as my executive secretary for a period of just over four months. During that time, Sally's duties included everything from balancing my personal checkbook to supervising my care following a heart attack. I can honestly say she excelled at every task presented to her and never balked at any assignment she was given, no matter how tough. Her loyalty to both me and my company never once wavered, though I'm sure there were times she wished my heart attack had killed me.
    It is with regret that I offer her the highest recommendation an employer can give an employee, as I'm quite certain I will find it impossible to secure a replacement with even half her secretarial skills or one who possesses a tenth of her heart.
    Sincerely,
    Vince Donnelly

Sally dropped the letter to her lap and simply stared. He'd written a letter of recommendation for her? Vince

Donnelly, the most insensitive and least considerate person she'd ever met? He'd even personally signed it, instead of using the signature stamp he often made her use when he didn't want to take the time to sign his correspondence. And she hadn't even requested a letter of recommendation from him!

She smoothed a hand over the page, touched by the thoughtfulness it represented, as much by the words he'd written.

Hauling in a breath, she stood and carried the letter to the kitchen and hung it on the refrigerator, using her favorite smiley-face magnet to hold it in place. She pressed a finger to her lips and touched it to his signature.

"Thanks, Vince," she whispered. "You'll never know how much this means to me."

The next morning Sally had the classified section of the newspaper spread open over her kitchen table, scanning for openings for a secretary, when her telephone rang. Snagging the receiver from the wall base, she said, "Hello?"

"Sally Gregg, please."

"This is she."

"Ms. Gregg, I'm Martha Starr, and I'm calling in reference to the outstanding balance on your Visa bill."

Sally's jaw sagged. "Are you kidding me? I just got the statement in yesterday's mail! It can't be overdue yet."

"Oh, no, ma'am," the woman assured her. "Your

payment isn't overdue. In fact, you don't owe us anything at all."

"That can't be right," Sally argued. "I should still owe at least two thousand dollars. I may only pay the minimum," she was quick to add, "but I'm never late with a payment and I keep accurate records of all my debts, so I know what my balance should be."

"Yes, ma'am. I can see that your payments have always arrived on time. The last was received yesterday morning in the amount of $2,003.95, which paid your account in full."

"No way!" Sally cried. "There must be a mistake. I haven't even paid the bill yet, much less paid it off."

"I have the information right here on my screen," the woman insisted. "The purpose of my call was to let you know the bill you received yesterday doesn't reflect the payment you made and—"

"I didn't make a payment!" Sally all but yelled.

"I'm sorry, ma'am," the woman said in confusion. "I don't know quite what to say. Your balance is zero."

Sally flattened her lips. "Don't worry. Someone in the proof department will catch the mistake tomorrow and realize a payment was posted to the wrong account." Heaving a sigh, she said, "Thanks for calling," and hung up the phone.

"Idiots," she muttered and started scanning the classifieds again.

The phone rang again and Sally was tempted not to answer it, sure it was the woman from Visa calling back to tell her they'd found the error and Sally's balance was the two thousand and something Sally had claimed it was in the first place.

On the third ring, she snatched up the phone. "Yes?" she said rudely.

"May I speak with Ms. Gregg, please?"

She clenched her jaw. "Speaking."

"I'm Doris, account manager for Union Chevrolet."

She rolled her eyes. "If you're calling me to tell me that my account is paid in full, you're wasting your time. I not only haven't *mailed* my payment, I'm not even sure I have the money in my bank account to cover the check when I do."

"Oh. Well. I'll have to discuss this with my supervisor. A mistake was made when your balance was figured and three cents remains outstanding. It's such a small amount, I'm sure my supervisor will approve my writing it off."

"Three cents?" she repeated. "Is that all you people think I owe you?" She tipped back her head and laughed. "Heck I'll pay the three cents. In fact, I'll give you a nickel and you can keep the change."

She hung up the phone while the woman was still talking, convinced that some hacker had released a monster virus that had attacked every computer system within the financial world and corrupted their records.

Which actually might be a good thing now that she thought about it. At least, it would be for her. It was bound to take a couple of days for the companies to restore all the lost data, which would buy her the extra time she needed to come up with the money to pay her bills.

"And pigs fly," she muttered, and picked up the classified section and began to scan again.

Vince stood before the windows in his den staring out. Darkness had settled over the landscape, and the only illumination came from the lights embedded in the pool walls. Bracing a hand against the window frame, he thought back over his day and felt a smile begin to spread on his face, as he imagined Sally's reaction if she knew all he'd done.

Saying good morning to Stacy had served as his warm-up, and from there he'd grown bolder with his attempts at finding his heart. He'd given Mark a raise and turned over the Holt account to him, with the promise of no intervention on his part. After lunch he'd dropped by the high school Mary's son attended and arranged for a scholarship for Jesse. The first semester Vince considered a gift, but from that point forward Jesse would earn the following semester's tuition by maintaining a 3.0 average. If he failed to produce the required grades…end of scholarship. In Vince's estimation, it was a fair deal and one he felt would better prepare Jesse for the future than if he were to just hand the kid the money with no expectations.

It was amazing what a few good deeds could do for a man. He'd charged through the day like the Energizer Bunny. It wasn't until six o'clock rolled around and he found himself alone at the office that he realized everything he'd accomplished wasn't enough. What he'd done was *good* and he *felt* good for having done it, but it hadn't cost him anything but money and he had more of that than he could spend in a lifetime. There was no sacrifice involved. It hadn't cost him anything. Not personally. And that was what Sally wanted from him, what she offered so freely. She gave of herself.

And that was what he was going to have to do. He was going to have to give until it hurt. Pull something from deep inside him that was going to cost him personally.

And he knew what that something was.

He was going to have to find that piece of paper and give it to Stephanie Parker.

Vince dragged a weary hand down his face, trying to think where else to search. He'd already gone through the safe at his house where he kept his family's records and dug through the boxes of his mother's he kept stored in his garage. He'd even driven back to the office and gone through the personal files he kept there and still hadn't found anything that even remotely resembled the torn piece of paper Sally had described.

Only one possibility remained.

His mother.

The thought of going to see her made him reevaluate his desire to find the missing piece of paper, as the visits were painful. She didn't recognize him any longer. Hadn't in almost a year. He hadn't visited her in months. It wasn't a conscious decision he'd made after careful consideration. He'd simply quit making the trip. He absolved himself of whatever guilt he might've felt by telling himself she didn't know whether he came or not.

She didn't recognize him, so what was the point of putting himself through the pain of seeing her, if she didn't know who he was?

He dropped his chin to his chest, knowing the answer before his conscience could remind him of the fact.

Because she's your mother.

Vince got an early start. It was a two-hour drive to the Alzheimer center where his mother lived, and he was anxious to find out if she knew anything about the piece of paper. He knew his chances of her remembering were slim. The one hope he clung to was that it pertained to his father, and Vincent Donnelly was the one person the disease hadn't erased from her mind.

When he entered her room and didn't see her, he thought for a moment she must be in the cafeteria eating her breakfast, or possibly at one of the many activities the staff scheduled throughout the day for their patients. But then he caught a glimpse of movement on the patio just outside the French doors and saw that she was sitting on a chair there, reading.

He kept his movements quiet as he opened the door and stepped outside, not wanting to startle her. He could only imagine how upsetting it must be to live in a world where you didn't recognize anyone, where every face you encountered was that of a stranger.

"Mom?" he called softly. "It's me. Vince."

She turned in her chair and looked at him. For the first time in over a year, the eyes that met his lit with recognition.

Smiling, she held out a hand. "Vince. Sweetheart, it's so good to see you."

He dropped to a knee and clasped her hand between his. "It's good to see you, too, Mom." He leaned to press a kiss on her cheek. When he started to withdraw, she placed a hand on his cheek and held his face before hers. "I swear you look more like your daddy every day."

He felt the old resentment rising and quickly shoved it back. "Since you always claimed he was the best-looking man in town, I'll take that as a compliment."

"And well you should." Smiling, she drew him around to face her. "So tell me what you've been doing with yourself? Still making money I'll bet."

"Yes, ma'am. Seems that's all I know how to do."

She slanted him a look. "Any women in your life?"

Sally popped into his mind, and he was tempted to tell his mother about her, then decided against it. He didn't want to chance confusing her and losing this rare moment of clarity. "No one special," he said vaguely.

She wagged a finger in his face. "You're my only chance at having grandchildren. If you don't get busy, I won't be around to spoil them."

He dropped his gaze, knowing if he did have children, she probably wouldn't recognize them when he brought them to visit. "I'll see what I can do, Mom."

She gave his hand a pat, then tugged at the blanket that covered her knees. When she did, the book she'd been reading slipped from her lap and fell to the patio. Vince stooped to pick it up. "What are you reading?"

A soft smile curved her lips. "The story of my life."

Vince flipped through a few pages. "I didn't know you kept a diary."

"Since I was a young girl." She laughed softly. "I've filled enough books over the years to outfit a library. This one," she said, with a nod at the book Vince held, "is the one I kept during my married life."

He continued to flip pages. "I had no idea." Something fell from the book and he stooped to pick it up…and found himself holding a torn piece of paper. Sure that he was looking at the piece of paper he'd searched so hard for, he lifted his gaze to his mothers.

"Do you know what this is?"

"Oh my, yes. Your father sent that to me when he was stationed in Vietnam. There's a story behind it. Would you like to hear it?"

Not trusting his voice, he nodded.

"It was just before your father left for Vietnam. He was in a bar in Austin, Texas, killing time while waiting for the flight that would take him overseas. There were several other soldiers with him. Six, counting your father. A man dropped by their table and offered to buy them all a drink. The soldiers agreed, but insisted he join them. As it turned out, the man had a son who'd served in Vietnam. Sadly, his son was killed only a few days before he was to come home.

"Now, your father never knew what possessed the man to do this, but the man took out a piece of paper and wrote out a bill of sale. When he finished, he tore the paper into six pieces and had each of the soldiers sign the back. A notary public, who was in the bar at the time, put her stamp on each piece making it official. Then the man told the soldiers to keep the piece he'd given to each of them, and when the war was over, they were to join the pieces together and bring them to him and he would give them his ranch."

Vince looked at her doubtfully, sure that she was either making up the story or Alzheimer's had claimed her mind again. Whichever the case, he'd probably never know.

"I know it's hard to believe," she said, as if sensing his doubt. "But that's the way your father told the story to me and he never was one to lie."

Smiling softly, she stroked a finger along the paper's faded edge. "This served as my talisman through the years. After your father died and when I was missing him the most, I would pull this out as a reminder of how lucky I was that he'd made it home from Vietnam at all when so many other men had lost their lives there. Those years we had with him after his return were truly a gift from God."

Her memories of that time were such a contrast to his own, Vince couldn't resist asking the question that had burned in his mind for years. "How did you stand it, Mom? Dad being gone all the time. Him giving away money, when we couldn't even pay our own bills?"

She tapped the piece of paper. "The secret's right here."

He searched her eyes, thinking the moment of lucidity had passed.

"When your father returned home," she explained, "he wasn't the same man I'd married. Not in a bad way," she was quick to add. "The war changed a lot of the soldiers, but it affected your father differently. He saw so much death over there, so much heartache. When he came home, he brought with him a desire to do something for the men who had died over there and those maimed by the war." She smiled proudly. "And he succeeded. I can't tell you the number of letters I've received over the years from families your father helped, and disabled veterans he stood by when no one else would."

Vince felt the resentment rising again, and this time he couldn't push it back. "But we needed him, too," he said angrily.

Her brow shot up, as if she were surprised that he would say such a thing. "But we had him, Vince. Your father made it home and all in one piece, while so many others didn't. How could we not share him with those who weren't as fortunate?" She laid her hand over the piece of paper. "Any time I felt resentment toward those he helped, all I had to do was pull this out and all my resentment would fade away."

Vince stared at the piece of paper he held, the one he'd searched for, driven hours to find, and realized now that he couldn't ask his mother to give up something that had given her so much comfort, no matter what it's possible worth. Opening the book, he slipped the piece of paper back between the pages. She laid a hand over his, stopping him before he could close the book.

"No, take it with you. You should have it now."

He shook his head. "No, Mom. I can't. It's yours."

She leaned to press a kiss on his forehead, then cupped a hand at his cheek and looked into his eyes. "I have no need for it any longer. It's time you experienced its gift."

Ten

By the time Vince reached the outskirts of Houston, he knew he had to see Sally. He'd probably never get past her front door, but he knew he had to try. The need to see her had grown stronger with each mile he'd driven. He wanted to tell her he'd found the piece of paper, share with her the story his mother had told him. Most of all he wanted to hold her. Tell her he loved her. Beg her to give him a chance to prove he wasn't the uncaring bastard she must think he was.

He knew where she lived now. After writing the recommendation for her, he'd had to pull her address from her employment records, in order to mail it to her. Now it was engraved in his mind.

He found the street easily enough, but was stunned

by the deplorable condition of the apartment complex in which she lived. Barefoot kids played a game of chase in the parking lot, weaving in and out of cars long past their prime. Teenage boys, their caps turned at a cocky angle, sat huddled on the stairs smoking cigarettes. Trash hugged the building's foundation, pushed there by the wind and left there by an inertia Vince had forgotten existed.

As he sat in his car in front of the building, he was both saddened and shamed to know she would choose to live in the midst of poverty and crime, rather than remain with him in his home.

Heaving a sigh, he approached her door and knocked.

"Just a sec!" he heard her call, then the door opened and she was there, a beam of sunshine in the shabbiness and desolation that surrounded him.

The welcoming smile she'd worn when opening the door slowly faded when she saw him.

"Vince."

Just seeing her was enough to rob him of the ability to speak, to think. He lifted a hand, wanting to touch her, but dropped it to his side, knowing he had no right.

She eased closer, her forehead creased in concern. "Is everything okay?"

He started to nod, then shook his head, knowing everything wasn't okay and hadn't been since the morning he'd woken up and found her gone.

"Vince, you're scaring me." Catching his hand, she pulled him inside and closed the door behind him. "Sit down," she said and urged him toward the sofa, before releasing his hand. "I'll get you something to drink."

He sank down on the sofa, grateful that he'd made it that far. While he waited for her to return, he looked around. The inside of her apartment was nothing like the outside of the building. The appliances and fixtures might be dated, but the place was clean as a whistle and all but burst with color.

He understood now why she'd said what she had about him needing a new interior designer. Though small, her home was a great deal more inviting than his more-spacious one. The furniture that filled it wasn't new, but it reflected the same warmth and comfort as the woman who had chosen it.

"Here."

He accepted the glass Sally handed him, sipped.

"Better?" she asked.

He nodded, then patted the seat next to him.

Though hesitant, she sank down beside him and drew a leg beneath her. "Is it your heart?" she asked in concern. "Are you having another attack?"

Chuckling, he set the glass aside. "No. There's nothing wrong with my heart. Not in the way you mean." He reached into his shirt pocket and pulled out the faded piece of paper.

Her eyes rounded, then shot to his. "You found it?"

He nodded. "It wasn't easy. I searched high and low both at home and at the office. I'd just about decided it didn't exist, when it occurred to me that my mother might have it, or at least know something about it."

Now that he'd found his voice, he couldn't seem to stop and continued on, anxious to share it all with Sally.

"I knew there was a strong chance she wouldn't be able to help me. Alzheimer's," he explained for her benefit. "Since she doesn't even know her own son, I didn't put much faith in her remembering a thirty-five-year-old scrap of paper."

She touched a hand to his arm. "I'm sorry. I know that must hurt. Your own mother, and she doesn't know you."

He gulped, remembering the emotion that had filled his throat when she'd turned to look at him and the recognition had lit in her eyes.

"She did today," he told her, then went on to explain. "I went to see her this morning and when I got there, she was sitting on the patio reading. To make a long story short, while we were talking, the book dropped from her lap. Not a book, really," he corrected. "More like a diary of her married life. Anyway, I picked up the book for her and the paper fell out."

She clapped a hand over heart. "Oh, my gosh! That gives me chills just hearing it."

"Did me, too," he admitted.

"Can I hold it?" she asked hopefully.

He passed it to her and watched as she examined both front and back.

Frowning, she looked up at him. "The words don't make any sense. Other than the back, of course. I assume that's your father's signature?"

"It's his, all right. My mother told me the story about how my dad came to have it. Want to hear it?"

She choked a laugh. "Just try leaving *without* telling me."

Feeling more at ease, he draped an arm along the back of the sofa between them. "It all goes back to the day my dad left for Vietnam."

He related the story to Sally just as his mother had told it to him. By the time he'd finished, tears filled her eyes.

"Oh, man," she said, fanning her face to keep from crying. "That's the most unbelievable story I've ever heard."

"I thought so, too."

She slanted him a questioning look. "You don't believe it?"

He shrugged. "I don't know whether I should or not. It's possible, I suppose." He tipped his head toward the paper she held. "Obviously someone gave it to him. That a rancher was the one is as likely an explanation as any other."

"So he planned to give them his ranch," she said thoughtfully.

"Seems that way, although I'd imagine that ranch is long gone by now. It's been over thirty-five years. A lot could have happened during that time. Mom said he had a son who was killed in Vietnam, so it's likely the man has passed on by now. Besides," he added, "Even if he really did intend to give his ranch to the soldiers, I'm sure he gave up on them claiming it long ago."

She flapped a dismissive hand. "The ranch isn't what this is about. It's the people and the story that surrounds it that are important."

That she'd feel that way didn't surprise Vince. Wealth and possessions meant nothing to Sally. People and matters of the heart were what she cared about.

"I've missed you, Sally."

The words were out before he realized he intended to say them.

She started to say something, then dropped her gaze. He'd swear he saw hope in her eyes, before she'd hidden them from him.

"I miss working for you, too, Vince."

"Sally." Taking a chance, he slid closer, his knee bumping hers. "Work isn't the only place I miss you. I miss you at my house, in my bed."

He saw the tears in her eyes and reached to lay a hand on her cheek. "I know you think I'm heartless and mean, and I don't blame you a bit for thinking that of me. I was that and worse. But I'm changing, Sally. I swear I am. I know it's not much, but I set up a scholarship for Mary's son, Jesse."

"Oh, Vince," she cried softly. "That's wonderful. I know Mary must be so grateful."

He shook his head. "She doesn't know. And won't," he added. "I set it up so that the school handles all the details. My name isn't involved at all. But the education is there for the boy if he wants it and is willing to work for it."

"He will," she assured. "All he needed was a chance."

He covered her hands with his. "I need one, too, Sally. The chance to prove to you that I'm changing, that I'm not the coldhearted man I was."

He watched the tears start to spill over and his heart

nearly broke. "Ah, Sal." Gathering her up, he pulled her onto his lap and held her close. "I'm so sorry I hurt you. I never meant to. I swear, I didn't. I love you, Sally. I want you, need you with me."

With tears streaming down her face, she placed a hand over his heart. "I didn't want to leave. I didn't. But I knew I couldn't live with a man who didn't care for me, respect me, my feelings."

He closed his hand over hers and held it tight against his heart. "But I do care for you. I love you. I know I've got a lot to learn about relationships, but I'm willing to try, if you'll just give me a chance to prove myself."

Smiling through her tears, she drew her hand from his to frame his face. "You don't have to prove anything to me, Vince. You already have. I know how much your father hurt you. I don't think he meant to, or was even aware of the pain he caused you, but the fact is he did."

She picked up the piece of paper she'd dropped and held it before his face. "Yet, you were willing to set aside whatever bitterness and resentment you felt toward him to find this. It's going to mean a lot to Stephanie Parker, as I'm sure it will the others involved, to know another part of the puzzle has been found. You've given them a gift, provided them with another link to their past."

He drew her hand to his lips. "Marry me, Sally, and be a part of my future."

Her eyes rounded. "*Marry* you?"

He pulled back to look at her. "Well, yeah. Did you think I came all the way over here looking for a roommate?"

Laughing, she threw her arms around his neck. "Roommate. Wife. I don't care, as long as I'm with you."

Just as quickly, she jerked back to look at him and narrowed her eyes. "It was you, wasn't it? You're the one who paid off my bills."

"Yes," he admitted. "And don't get all in a huff about it. It wasn't right that you got stuck with your ex's debt." He lifted a shoulder. "I was just balancing the scales a bit."

"Oh, Vince."

She melted against him and kissed him, the paper she still clutched brushing his cheek. He'd swear he sensed the power in it, the history, the love that was pressed into it over the years by his mother's hands. Like the others who had possessed similar pieces to the puzzle, he doubted the paper would ever be of any value.

But to Vince his piece was worth all the gold in the world, because he knew, without its help, he would never have stood a chance of winning Sally's love.

* * * * *

Watch for the next book in Peggy Moreland's
A PIECE OF TEXAS *series,*
THE TEXAN'S SECRET PAST,
on sale this August form Silhouette Desire.

Mediterranean Nights

Join the guests and crew of **Alexandra's Dream,**
*the newest luxury ship to set sail on the
romantic Mediterranean, as they experience
the glamorous world of cruising.*

*A new Harlequin continuity series
begins in June 2007 with
FROM RUSSIA, WITH LOVE
by Ingrid Weaver*

*Marina Artamova books a cabin on the luxurious
cruise ship* **Alexandra's Dream,** *when she finds
out that her orphaned nephew and his adoptive
father are aboard. She's determined to be
reunited with the boy…but the romantic ambience
of the ship and her undeniable attraction to
a man she considers her enemy are about
to interfere with her quest!*

Turn the page for a sneak preview!

Piraeus, Greece

"THERE SHE IS, Stefan. *Alexandra's Dream*." David Anderson squatted beside his new son and pointed at the dark blue hull that towered above the pier. The cruise ship was a majestic sight, twelve decks high and as long as a city block. A circle of silver and gold stars, the logo of the Liberty Cruise Line, gleamed from the swept-back smokestack. Like some legendary sea creature born for the water, the ship emanated power from every sleek curve—even at rest it held the promise of motion. "That's going to be our home for the next ten days."

The child beside him remained silent, his cheeks working in and out as he sucked furiously on his thumb.

Hair so blond it appeared white ruffled against his forehead in the harbor breeze. The baby-sweet scent unique to the very young mingled with the tang of the sea.

"Ship," David said. "Uh, *parakhod.*"

From beneath his bangs, Stefan looked at the *Alexandra's Dream.* Although he didn't release his thumb, the corners of his mouth tightened with the beginning of a smile.

David grinned. That was Stefan's first smile this afternoon, one of only two since they had left the orphanage yesterday. It was probably because of the boat—according to the orphanage staff, the boy loved boats, which was the main reason David had decided to book this cruise. Then again, there was a strong possibility the smile could have been a reaction to David's attempt at pocket-dictionary Russian. Whatever the cause, it was a good start.

The liaison from the adoption agency had claimed that Stefan had been taught some English, but David had yet to see evidence of it. David continued to speak, positive his son would understand his tone even if he couldn't grasp the words. "This is her maiden voyage. Her first trip, just like this is our first trip, and that makes it special." He motioned toward the stage that had been set up on the pier beneath the ship's bow. "That's why everyone's celebrating."

The ship's official christening ceremony had been held the day before and had been a closed affair, with only the cruise-line executives and VIP guests invited, but the stage hadn't yet been disassembled. Banners bearing the blue and white of the Greek flag of the ship's owner, as well as the Liberty circle of stars logo, draped the edges of the platform. In the center, a group of musicians and a dance troupe dressed in traditional white folk costumes performed for the benefit of the *Alexandra's Dream*'s first passengers. Their audience was in a festive mood, snapping their fingers in time to the music while the dancers twirled and wove through their steps.

David bobbed his head to the rhythm of the mandolins. They were playing a folk tune that seemed vaguely familiar, possibly from a movie he'd seen. He hummed a few notes. "Catchy melody, isn't it?"

Stefan turned his gaze on David. His eyes were a striking shade of blue, as cool and pale as a winter horizon and far too solemn for a child not yet five. Still, the smile that hovered at the corners of his mouth persisted. He moved his head with the music, mirroring David's motion.

David gave a silent cheer at the interaction. Hopefully, this cruise would provide countless opportunities for more. "Hey, good for you," he said. "Do you like the music?"

The child's eyes sparked. He withdrew his thumb with a pop. *"Moozika!"*

"Music. Right!" David held out his hand. "Come on, let's go closer so we can watch the dancers."

Stefan grasped David's hand quickly, as if he feared it would be withdrawn. In an instant his budding smile was replaced by a look close to panic.

Did he remember the car accident that had killed his

parents? It would be a mercy if he didn't. As far as David knew, Stefan had never spoken of it to anyone. Whatever he had seen had made him run so far from the crash that the police hadn't found him until the next day. The event had traumatized him to the extent that he hadn't uttered a word until his fifth week at the orphanage. Even now he seldom talked.

David sat back on his heels and brushed the hair from Stefan's forehead. That solemn, too-old gaze locked with his, and for an instant, David felt as if he looked back in time at an image of himself thirty years ago.

He didn't need to speak the same language to understand exactly how this boy felt. He knew what it meant to be alone and powerless among strangers, trying to be brave and tough but wishing with every fiber of his being for a place to belong, to be safe, and most of all for someone to love him….

He knew in his heart he would be a good parent to Stefan. It was why he had never considered halting the adoption process after Ellie had left him. He hadn't balked when he'd learned of the recent claim by Stefan's spinster aunt, either; the absentee relative had shown up too late for her case to be considered. The adoption was meant to be. He and this child already shared a bond that went deeper than paperwork or legalities.

A seagull screeched overhead, making Stefan start and press closer to David.

"That's my boy," David murmured. He swallowed hard, struck by the simple truth of what he had just said.

That's my *boy*.

"I CAN'T BE PATIENT, RUDOLPH. I'm not going to stand by and watch my nephew get ripped from his country and his roots to live on the other side of the world."

Rudolph hissed out a slow breath. "Marina, I don't like the sound of that. What are you planning?"

"I'm going to talk some sense into this American kidnapper."

"No. Absolutely not. No offence, but diplomacy is not your strong suit."

"Diplomacy be damned. Their ship's due to sail at five o'clock."

"Then you wouldn't have an opportunity to speak with him even if his lawyer agreed to a meeting."

"I'll have ten days of opportunities, Rudolph, since I plan to be on board that ship."

* * * * *

Follow Marina and David as they join forces to uncover the reason behind little Stefan's unusual silence, and the secret behind the death of his parents....

Look for From Russia, With Love
by Ingrid Weaver
in stores June 2007.

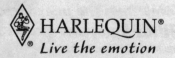

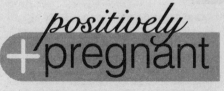

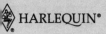

COMING NEXT MONTH

#1801 FORTUNE'S FORBIDDEN WOMAN—Heidi Betts
Dakota Fortunes
Can he risk the family honor to fulfill an unrequited passion with the one woman he's forbidden to have?

#1802 SIX-MONTH MISTRESS—Katherine Garbera
The Mistresses
She was contracted to be his mistress in exchange for his help in getting her struggling business off the ground. Now he's come to collect his prize.

#1803 AN IMPROPER AFFAIR—Anna DePalo
Millionaire of the Month
This ruthless businessman is on the verge of extracting the ultimate revenge…until he falls for the woman who could jeopardize his entire plan.

#1804 THE MILLIONAIRE'S INDECENT PROPOSAL—Emilie Rose
Monte Carlo Affairs
When an attractive stranger offers her a million euros to become his mistress, will she prove his theory that everyone has a price?

#1805 BETWEEN THE CEO'S SHEETS—Charlene Sands
She'd been paid off to leave him. Now he wants revenge and will stop at nothing until he settles the score…and gets her back in his bed.

#1806 RICH MAN'S REVENGE—Tessa Radley
He'd marry his enemy's daughter and extract his long-denied revenge—but his new bride has her own plan for him.